I AM JOHN SULLIVAN: BOOK 1

Chapter 1: Purge

I enjoyed my sausage and eggs as I watched Mr. Smith battle with the throes of his previous decisions through the monitor sitting at my kitchen table. I had attached chains around his wrist and neck, leaving him hanging naked in my basement while the rising heat of a portable camping-cooker seared his bound feet. He would pull his legs up toward his abdomen, or hold them out to the sides, but the exhaustion after three hours had taken its toll. His once milky-white feet were now charred black and littered with blisters.

I had first encountered Mr. Smith or "Jerry" as I came to know him, four months prior while I was out at a nearby bar. I was alone, drinking heavily as I so often did, trying to block out the ever increasing pace of my racing thoughts.

While sitting alone on my barstool sipping whisky and staring off into space, a pale man with thinning grey hair, a large hooked nose, and a sickly smile came and sat next to me. He looked to be in his early fifties and was dressed in dirty jeans and a flannel shirt. He was a typical white trash mutant that resided in the local area. I had met many just like him, or so I thought. I tried to ignore him and tune him out, thinking he would walk away, but he was the kind of guy who just couldn't take a hint.

He went on and on about women, not knowing when he would be laid off from his construction job, and how sick he was of paying child support to his whore ex-wife. After a while I decided just to play along. He offered a distraction that complimented my excessive whisky consumption. We ended up talking for over three hours; taking shot after shot, and drinking the night away.

I encountered Jerry several more times at the same bar. I would stop in three or four nights a week, and almost every time he had mysteriously shown up. It became clear that he knew my vehicle and that he would drive by to see if it was out in the parking lot. He was there too often for it to simply be coincidence.

Each time we spoke he would jest that we were becoming best friends, that he trusted me, and that I was wise for my young age. After a while the conversations became more personal. As the whisky flowed he began to offer up information that he would soon realize should have been kept a secret.

He told me that there was a girls only catholic school not far from his house. Jerry went on about how he would hide in the woods with a video camera and record the young girls as they passed by.

After he had captured significant material he would take it back to his trailer and enhance the footage on his computer. He leaned in close and, in a whispered tone, said that he would strip himself naked and then masturbate to the footage while his feet were sitting in a tub of ice water. Apparently the sensation from the cold allowed him a more powerful climax.

My stomach turned as he went on, but I encouraged him to do so. I needed to know exactly what his ailment consisted of so that I could better decide his fate. He went on, saying that he was considering approaching one of the girls, and that he was working on new ways to intensify his pleasures. He had begun wearing panties while pleasing himself, and said he wanted a pair from one of the girls. He told me that even discussing it was exciting and that if I wanted to, I could join him in both the recording and the masturbation process.

As he went on, night after night, expanding upon the details of it all, I knew that he had to be executed. Though he said he had not touched one of the children yet, it would only be a matter of time before he could no longer control his urges; before he stole the innocence from one of the girls.

Last night I'd asked him if he wanted to join me at my house for some drinks after the bar closed, and drunkenly he had accepted my offer. I sensed that he wanted to engage in sexual activity as we walked back to my vehicle. He became flirtatious, complementing me, telling me that my beard made me look strong, like Charlton Heston in his prime. I knew this was a form of flattery, as Charlton was much more handsome than I.

He had told me many times before that he had not had sex in over three years, since his wife left him, and that he was desperate for companionship. He trusted me, and felt that I understood his twisted mind. If only he had known what he was walking into, surely his words would not have been so kind.

After entering the kitchen of my home he tried to make an advance, rubbing my shoulders and asking if I'd like a massage. I was sickened by his touch, but remained calm, as that could be used to my advantage. I told him to wait just a bit longer, that we should have a drink first. I poured a glass of whiskey for each of us and then raised a toast.

"To a wonderful friendship, and who knows... maybe more."

He responded by taking down the entire glass in one gulp, then wiped his chin with the back of his hand like the pig that he was. I only took a small sip from my own glass, just as I had been doing at the bar. He had become too intoxicated to realize that I was fully sober, and that I was playing him.

We sat and talked for another fifteen minutes, and as each minute passed I could see the final glass of whisky taking control of him. His eyes squinted as he slurred and stumbled over every word. He asked if he could use the restroom, as he thought he was going to be sick. I pointed toward the hallway telling him to take his time, and that I would be in shortly to check up on him. He thanked me as he headed down the hall.

After seeing the door shut I grabbed the crowbar I kept beneath the kitchen sink and headed in after him. When I opened the door he was on his hands and knees vomiting into the toilet. As I approached him his eyes met my own, and through his drunken haze saw that I had the weapon in my hand. He screamed in terror as I raised the crowbar above my head, and then silence fell over the room as I cracked him on top of the head, opening a deep gash and exposing his skull.

I then placed his head in a duffel bag and zipped it up to his neck to contain any further vomit or blood, reducing the cleanup that would later take place. I drug him through the house by his feet, and down the stairway into the basement where he would be chained, left hanging by the rafters until my return.

After finishing my breakfast I headed back down to meet with Jerry again. He cried out, begging me to let him go as I shut off the cooker beneath his feet, but no one would hear him. I had sound proofed the entire basement with foam and insulation. It was very expensive and time consuming, yet necessary. Ignoring him, I walked over to my workbench and picked up the stereo remote. After selecting a nineteen fifties rock-compilation and turning the volume up to max, I picked out the first tool to be used.

I had recently purchased a corkscrew and was eager to test it out. After putting on the surgical mask, rubber apron, and elbow length gloves from the janitorial bin next to the workbench, I held the tool up to Jerry's face so that he could see it with full clarity.

As I placed the pointed tip on the middle of his left thigh, Mr. Smith asked what I was going to do. His lips quivered, and his eyes, crusted with mucus and tears from the previous fiery torture, blinked rapidly in fearful anticipation. I answered him, my voice devoid of emotion.

"I am going to drive this into your flesh, turn it until it will go no further, and then... rip it out."

He squirmed and protested, promising me money, and that he wouldn't go to the police if I let him down. I disregarded his impossible request, as all the money in the world, something a man like him would never be able to acquire, simply wouldn't be enough, and replied...

"If you try to fight me, or pull away from the screw, I am going to cut off your cock and make you swallow it. Do you understand?" He screamed and begged as the words passed my lips.

"Please... don't do this! I'm sorry for whatever I did... please... John!"

He was clearly not taking the ordeal seriously. I had to show him the consequences of his actions, that I was in control, and that he must do as I say, or suffer. Taking the tailor shears from my work bench I lifted his penis upwards with a gloved hand, and with no hesitation, cut off about a quarter of the head. He howled from the excruciating pain, calling for his God to help him as the scissors came to a close.

I stood before him as he writhed; waiting for the right moment, knowing from experience that it was near. As Jerry sucked in air rapidly, hyperventilating and drooling, his mouth gaped open. I took the piece of flesh and jammed it into the back of his throat. He gagged and snapped at my fingers with his teeth, but I had already removed them from his mouth. Forcefully I grabbed the top of his head with one hand, and held his mouth shut with the other, giving him one final warning.

"I am going to let you spit this out, but the next time you interrupt me, you will not have the option. Do as I say."

After releasing my hands, Jerry spit the flesh onto the floor and began to dry heave, as he was severely dehydrated at that point.

As I drove the corkscrew into his thigh he faded in and out of consciousness. His body was trying to find ways to cope with the pain, but I wouldn't allow that to last. After the screw was twisted into his leg, all the way to the hilt, I slapped him and shouted out his name, bringing him back to the reality that awaited him.

"Jerry, are you ready for me to remove this from your thigh? Don't be afraid, you can answer me now."

"John… Don't do this… Don't kill me! I swear… whatever I've done… I'll fix it… You don't have to do this!"

Annoyed by his response I ripped and pulled at the corkscrew handle, and slowly his meat shredded apart, yet some remained on the tip of the utensil as it exited his thigh. Jerry's torso flailed about as he fought against the chains. His legs shook violently and mucus dripped from his nose, but he did not try to pull away. He had taken my threat seriously.

Working the metal out of his flesh had sweat dripping from my brow. I sat down on my workbench and examined Jerry for about ten minutes, giving my muscles a chance to recover. He looked pathetic. His body was thin, but not in a healthy way. He lacked any sort of muscle tone and loose skin hung from his chest and lower abdomen. He had drank himself into nothing. I knew that if I did not stop my excessive drinking I too would end up with a pitiful body that had given up on me. However, Jerry had about thirty years of alcohol use under his belt; I had only been consistent for the last two, and was significantly younger than he was. I had time to find a substitute, a medication to numb my mind.

I then began to question the man hanging before me.

"Jerry, I want you to be straight with me... Did you ever touch one of the children you told me about? Do not lie to me, Jerry; I'll know if you do."

"John! I swear man... I never did, I just took the videos... I even deleted most of them... I'm not that sick! I wouldn't hurt a child... I have children of my own... Please man... Please! I was fucking lonely... I told you that my wife left me... Come on man!"

He sobbed and whimpered, going on about how much he missed his own children, how much they needed him, how he was innocent. It was pathetic.

I didn't believe him. He had to understand the magnitude of what he had done. He had to feel the pain he had brought upon the innocent. I picked up the fishing knife from my workbench and began filleting his genitals as I sang along with Elvis, who was blaring out of the stereo speakers. Jerry's bound feet cramped up tightly and he tried to push me away with his knees, but he was too weak, there was nothing he could do.

After removing most of the flesh from his nether regions I held the knife up to his right eye and told him:

"I am going to put the items in my left hand inside of your mouth. When I do, you will swallow them. If you spit them out onto the floor I am going to remove your eye and make you eat that as well. Do you understand, Jerry?"

He screamed and lamented for long moments, refusing to look at me or answer my question.

Growing tired of his hollering and whimpering prayers to God I gagged him with his genitals and taped his mouth shut. Looking over my instrument table I selected carefully. I had ordered a medical saw from the internet a few months before, but had yet to test it out. I decided that removing his feet, starting at the lower shin bone would be the next step.

As I cut I reminisced on the times we'd spent together at the bar. As he went on and on with stories about his wife cheating, and how pretty the young girls were, I would sit relaxed, pretending to be interested, and dream of that moment. The moment I would be able to rip him apart.

After I had removed each foot, I stopped the blood flow with a tourniquet and sealed the wounds with a blow torch. I was running out of time. Jerry had lost a lot of blood. His body wouldn't be able to handle much more. It was time to finish the task.

His head rocked back and forth and his eyes were glassy and distant.

"Jerry… Jerry, look at me. Are you ready to die now?"

He pouted, and though his mouth was stuffed, refusing to swallow his own manhood, I could still make out a pathetic and muffled "please…"

I was content with his response. At least he was still conscious enough to know that I would be his end. I picked up the long-handle-axe I'd bought from the hardware store and began chopping away at his body. I was in no particular rush at that point, nor did I care in what order my blows landed. After the fifth slice into his torso he stopped responding. There was no more quivering, grunting, or convulsions. I had completed the task. I had absolved Jerry of his sins. However, I still needed to dispose of the body and clean up any DNA left behind.

I had ordered four barrels of sulfuric acid about a month prior to Jerry's execution, but the paperwork, the forgery… the whole ordeal had been very time consuming, and a slow process. I wouldn't have the barrels for quite some time. I just had to make do with what I had.

The method I had been using, which required a great deal of effort, was the best option. I cut Jerry down into sixteen pieces so that he would fit into the wood burning stove I'd picked up from an antique auction a while back. It was difficult to move it down into the basement, as it weighed over four-hundred pounds. Hooking up the chimney hadn't been enjoyable either, but the effort was well worth it.

The smell of burning human flesh is distinct, and though there were not many in the western world who knew that smell, I still had to be very careful. I only burned bodies after ten p.m. on weeknights. I used three bags of charcoal, five bottles of lighter fluid, and a quarter chord of wood. The process took about seven hours to reduce all of the flesh to ash, and then I had to get rid of the bones.

With an electric saw I cut what remained of the charred and brittle bones up into several pieces, and then smashed them into a fine powder with a smithy hammer. Slowly I flushed it all down the toilet. It took me over an hour, but the danger of clogging the lines and having to call a plumber reinforced my patience. The water bill would be outrageously high, but until I had the acid that was the best method.

After the body was successfully disposed of I burned the plastic tarp that had been beneath Jerry's hanging body. The next step was always the most tedious. First I had to strip naked and toss both Jerry's, and my own clothing into the wood-burning stove. Then my skin, my hair, and everything else were washed with bleach. Both the basement and the first floor had to be mopped and scrubbed as well. Every counter, every door, and every tool I had used... anything that Jerry could have possibly come in contact with; they all had to be cleansed.

Once the process was complete I took a twenty minute shower followed by a hot bath. After toweling off I sat naked at my computer desk, a bottle of whisky at my side, and drank myself into a peaceful coma, eventually passing out on the floor.

Chapter 2: Duality

God damn I need a drink I muttered to myself. Sluggishly I rose to the sound of my nagging alarm clock. The blue numbers flashed three p.m. and the electric buzzing stung my eardrums like salt on an open wound. As I sat up my lower back ached and my left shoulder screamed in agony. Years of physical labor and bodily abuse had created a lot of unneeded friction within my joints. I could still fully function, well, for the most part, but the pain was always there. Surely the excessive alcohol consumption, lack of sleep, and poor food choices were not helping.

I had recently read an article written by a doctor who boasted the effectiveness of unorthodox medical practices. He claimed that sleeping on the floor could cure lower back pain by straightening the spine, so I decided to try it. I have to admit that it had helped, but it left me with a stuffy nose and my mouth always tasted like rust when I rose from my slumber.

Gritting my teeth, I used my uninjured right arm to get to my feet. My knees popped as I stood and I was momentarily lightheaded. I couldn't seem to recall feeling like that when I was a child. I was only twenty-nine and felt like my body was already quitting on me.

Slight nausea from the bottle of whisky I had finished off before passing out clouded my brain and stirred in my gut. I knew through repetition that taking a fifteen minute shower, brushing my teeth twice for two minutes each time, and chugging exactly thirty-two ounces of water with my generic multivitamin would mask my temporary ailment enough to drive to work.

I swatted at the light switch with a lazy hand as I entered the bathroom and walked over to the mirror, silently praying to no one in particular that my athletic body would appear. As many times before, I was disappointed. My torso was a bit flabby and my tattoos didn't look so cool anymore. Though I was discontent with my new figure I had found ways to deal with it. Those ways consisted of wearing bigger t-shirts and walking with my gut sucked in and my chest puffed out. I didn't even know why I cared. I suppose the only logical reason is that I wanted to appear normal to the outside world. Not just normal, but as someone who had respect for himself.

After studying my fat body I sighed and made my way to the shower. I'd come to the conclusion that letting it run for one minute lets it get just warm enough. The temperature was not maxed out yet, but it was also not so cold that I couldn't handle it. That first minute was exactly enough time to chug thirty-two ounces of water out of the plastic fast food cup I kept on the counter next to the multivitamin.

Upon entering the shower I liked to start things off by wetting my hair and my beard, letting the water drip down slowly so that it would prime the rest of my body for soap. First in line was the dual purpose shampoo. It was not only a shampoo, but a conditioner as well. I chose this because it saved both time and money. I discovered that wonderful product after getting dandruff for the first time. That happened eight years ago when I moved from Texas to New Jersey and experienced a serious climate change. I was annoyed, as it started to flake while I was at work. I suffered through four days of dandruff; four days of appearing unclean before I figured out that conditioner alone would not be enough. I needed dual action, medical grade scalp solution.

I emptied out about three ounces of the concoction into my open hand even though the back of the bottle said to squirt a nickel size circle onto your palm. Those instructions had always bewildered me. How small does one's head have to be… how thin does one's hair have to be for that amount to suffice? I honestly couldn't answer that question because I had a fully developed cranium, and by way of good genetics, a fairly thick mane of hair. I always used a lot of soap because I needed to smell sanitary. Knowing that others secretly approved of my aroma was necessary as it assured me that I would be well received by all.

As I rubbed the milky dual action shampoo through my mane and my beard I was reminded that I was well overdue for a haircut, and that I needed to shave. For years I was clean-cut with a high and tight look, however, in the previous six months or so I'd decided that a few inches of hair with a mildly burly biker-beard was more suitable, more daring. It better projected the persona I wanted the world to see. Unfortunately, I looked more like a young Santa Clause than a Hells Angel.

I knew that when I finished bathing, I would look in the mirror again and cringe at how foolish I must have looked to others, but I knew I just needed to hang in there a little longer. The image I had settled on would eventually conform to me, and people would start to see the rebellious, yet law-abiding biker-type instead of the chubby gift giver.

I liked to leave the dual action shampoo in my hair and in my beard while I scrubbed myself with the body sponge I'd bought recently. It came highly recommended by a metro-sexual oriented magazine I read while waiting at the dentist. I wasn't overly opposed to just using a bar of soap, but I was opposed to not being as clean as possible. Perhaps it was a fine paradox.

It had been proven that a course sponge saturated with anti-bacterial body wash cleaned much deeper than a bar would. It also saved time and money, just like my dual action shampoo did. I felt like I had an advantage of sorts because I knew there were other people out there who still used soap bars. I was saving nearly seventy dollars a year over someone who chose the bar and wash cloth method. Pubic hair also got stuck in soap bars, and the people who used it were rubbing it all over their naked flesh. Who would want soiled genital hair stuck in their soap bar and rubbed all over their body? I knew I didn't.

Sighing loudly I shut the water off and grabbed my towel. For reasons unknown it had become a hassle for me. It wasn't that drying my body off was difficult; I just didn't like doing it. After finishing the tedious task, I walked back over to the sink and loaded up my toothbrush with whitening toothpaste. I had been using whitening toothpaste for almost eight years, and my teeth were still the same shade of pearl. Perhaps it was just preserving my color. It cost more than standard toothpaste, but I feared that if I didn't use it my teeth would start to turn yellow. That was a risk I was not willing to take.

The medium grade dentist recommended brush felt amazing against my gums. I liked to move my hand in circular motions while rapidly scrubbing back and forth. My dentist said that that was not the best method for cleaning, but I thought he was wrong. I didn't enjoy the company of my dentist. He had one of those creepy permanent smiles and, ironically, horrifically bad breath. I often thought he should try taking up my stroking technique, it may have helped him with his odious case of halitosis.

I always saved brushing my tongue for last. It was the most important part of the ritual when it came to destroying bad breath. I didn't save it for last because it was the most important though. I saved it for last because it could be vomit inducing for a hung-over alcoholic. I knew that I was guaranteed to gag a minimum of four times between the two, two minute brushing sessions. However, it had to be done. I couldn't possibly leave my home if I didn't do it. I had to be the essence of antiseptic if I was to face the general public.

After brushing twice I always rinsed thoroughly with mouth wash. It was a green colored generic brand and tasted like acidic cheap chewing gum. I kept it in my mouth for the next two minutes while I moved on to the next step in my morning ritual.

If there were a top five percent of fastest dressers in the world I would be among them. I could usually go from naked to fully clothed, with shoes on, in less than forty-five seconds. I could do that because I was naturally fast and extremely decisive. My service in the military had perfected the technique, bringing it to the highest level.

Once the transformation from naked to fully clothed was complete I headed back into the bathroom and put on my gel based deodorant. It seemed more logical to apply the antiperspirant before putting on a shirt, but I didn't.

I had seen a horrible eighties film a few years before, and in that movie a man with a ridiculous looking mullet and stone washed jeans was rushed for work and ended up lifting his shirt and putting on the deodorant before running out the door. He came off as an important person, like a man who did not have enough time in the day to take care of all of his obligations. I started emulating the procedure every single day, though I had added slight modifications to it. I felt like that process made my time more valuable and that my contributions to society would be more likely recognized as selfless acts. People would sense that I was willing to multi-task in the morning in order to make time for them.

After application I stared into the mirror expressionless, slowly raising and lowering my arms. That forced the deodorant into the pours of my underarms, essentially guaranteeing that I would not have body odor later on in the day. I also liked the remaining residual deodorant to brush against my cotton shirt, complimenting my excellent smell, and providing an additional blanket of security.

With ten seconds left on the clock for my oral rinsing I left my room and made my way down the stairs, skipping the first two steps, changing hand position on the railing, and then hitting every other step with short, choppy, deliberate stomps. As soon as I hit the first floor I began walking at a brisk pace through the dining room, and then the kitchen, all while being on my heels. I reached the side door and in one fluid motion unlocked it, opened it, slid through it, locked it, and slammed the door behind me, just in time to spit the mouth wash out into the grass.

Tilting my head back I gasped for air as I had been breathing through my stuffy nose for the previous two minutes. At that time one of the local non English speaking Mexicans walked past my driveway slowly and stared at me with his dark eyes and pursed lips as if I was crazy. If anything, he was the crazy one. It was nearly ninety degrees outside and he was wearing a long sleeve orange shirt with cartoon characters on it. What the fuck did he know?

There in my driveway, only a few feet in front of me sat my brand new middle class luxury sedan. I studied it carefully, taking special note of the way the sun gleamed off of the high gloss, smoky-black paint job. I was also content with the brushed aluminum rims. They were eighteen inches and looked to be of high quality.

I'd been told on multiple occasions that such a prestigious vehicle did not mesh well with my stern personality type and blue collar clothing style. Some said I should have gotten a big truck, or even an American muscle car. I knew two things that they did not. The first thing was that I did not suffer from the medical condition known as micro-penis, and did not believe that having a big or loud vehicle would enhance my size. The second thing was the specific reason I had bought the car.

I'd always wanted to be normal. It was a journey that I had failed at miserably since I began it at the age of thirteen. I needed to buy a vehicle that would tell the world a few things about me. I needed people to know that I chose to drive a car that met the highest emission standards, explaining without words that I cared for the environment. The price and overall quality of the vehicle highlighted that I was both a successful middle-class American, and a man who knew and appreciated the value of a dollar.

After careful consideration I decided to go with the v-6 to send a specific message to onlookers. It made the statement that although I was almost thirty years old; I still enjoyed a bit of power under the hood and probably had a slight edge to me. I had thought about getting the package with the supercharger, but through tedious calculation, I knew that I would come off as a man overcompensating for something, and that something would likely be a man trying to camouflage the fact that his penis length was meager at best. Overall I felt like that vehicle was the perfect choice for a man who projected confidence, professionalism, and a hint of style.

With one final look at the smoky-black beauty before me, I walked around to the driver's side and entered my prized means of conveyance. I had chosen the two-tone titanium interior, as it was very sleek and stayed cool in the summer time. If I was ever to have a passenger in my vehicle, I wanted them to appreciate my taste and know that I had an eye for quality.

After buckling my seatbelt and checking both the rearview and side mirrors twice I put the car in reverse and made my way down the long asphalt driveway. I had to be extremely careful during that time. Where I lived, there was an abundance of self-absorbed streetwalkers who traveled at a very slow pace and had absolutely no consideration for vehicles, or the basic laws of traffic. I had lost count of how many times I had almost hit one of those mutants.

That day must have been a slow one for the nearly homeless, as none of the creatures were blocking the path of the driveway that I paid for. As I entered the street I put the car into drive and began the ten minute journey to work. While traveling down the trash riddled road toward the stoplight, the usual wave of discontent forced a sigh passed my lips. I couldn't avert my eyes from the piece of shit cars with big shiny rims that lined either side of the road, or the town drunk and his party of layman's who sat on his porch for fifteen hours each day, smoking cigarettes and drinking cheap beer; all on the government's dollar.

I rarely broke routine, and on that day I certainly wouldn't. Just before the stoplight at the end of the street there was a convenient store on the left side of the road. I pulled in slowly and parked as far away from the other cars as possible. After exiting the vehicle I walked straight toward the filthy double doors leading into the Mecca of lottery tickets and junk food.

As I swung the door open, blatantly trying to avoid contact with any area near the handle, a typical dreg of poor American society walked past me, carelessly challenging me with his cantankerous eyes and broken English, stating "scuse me mane" as he intentionally rubbed his shoulder against mine to show his dominance.

I ignored the slug, checking my rage and recognizing that his entire life had probably consisted of negative reinforcement from his single parent home. He had no idea what it was like to be told that he had done a good job, nor did he realize that in a cosmic sense his life force was as equally insignificant as my own.

Insecurities surely tore at his soul day in and day out, and the chances were very high that he would pass on his self-hating gene to a fatherless child one day, that is, if he had not done so already.

My train of thought was interrupted as I approached the line of freezers located on the back wall of the store. I opened the creaking door with the broken seal and selected my favorite energy drink. Twenty four ounces of nuclear colored cough syrup, loaded with vitamins, ridiculous amounts of caffeine, and who really knew what else. I needed that concoction. I was at least one hundred percent more productive while under its influence. I grabbed three just in case there was a heavy workload ahead of me. Smashing a hammer against metal while hopped up on legalized liquid cocaine was exhilarating.

I approached the cashier, refusing eye contact with the other customers and placed my items on the counter. The clerk turned around and I was pleased to see it was the owner of the store. He was a Korean man in his mid to late thirties. He spoke elegantly, took pride in his professionalism, and performed his duties very well.

He nodded at me and I nodded back before asking for one can of smokeless tobacco. He had seen me, and I had seen him roughly four-hundred times in the last two years. I came to the store often, and sensed that he felt as if he knew me, and I shared that sentiment.

His eyes squinted suspiciously as he spoke to me.
"I thought you gave this up?" Slightly ashamed I answered as politely as my unenthusiastic monotone voice would allow.

"Yeah man, I thought I did, but I needed something extra to temporarily bring balance and structure back into my life."

At first he looked perplexed by my response, but then changed his expression to one of understanding and nodded empathetically. I paid the man and wished him well as I exited the store.

As soon as I was safely buckled into my seat, I chugged down an entire energy drink and put a tiny bag of tobacco between my bottom lip and gum. I pulled out of the parking lot and luckily made it through the light before it turned red.

It was time for the best eight minutes of my day to begin. I fiddled with the buttons located on the center dash and brought the vehicle to a comfortable temperature. Then I pressed the play button on my stereo and seventies rock blared out of my speakers. I felt a rush of adrenaline course through my veins as I gripped the steering wheel tightly and visualized myself strangling my next victim.

I did not want to alarm the vehicles passing me by who seemed to think five under the speed limit was too slow to deal with, so I kept my head banging and jaw clinching to a bare minimum and quietly mouthed the lyrics to the current song. After the surge died down I relaxed and fell into a rhythm. My mind expanded and thoughts began to pour out of my frontal lobe and take hold of my spirit. My inner being was transforming as the electricity and delicate chemicals that made it all possible crashed together in the host that we call a body.

I began going over possible problematic scenarios that I may encounter at work and started throwing solutions at them as they came to me. I knew that remaining calm and giving those that I trusted the benefit of the doubt was the first step and a good start to most situations. However, if there was an emergency that called for immediate impulsive action, it was imperative that I have a sound game plan ready.

As that thought occurred I searched through my memory bank and located every fire extinguisher, eye wash station, and first aid kit within my work center. I went over the procedures for CPR and the step by step directing of bystanders to ensure success. One could never be too careful, nor did one know when disaster would strike. It was my duty as not only a good Samaritan, but as a human being to be emotionally ready and physically able to handle whatever came my way when it dealt with the preservation of innocent life.

Perhaps that was too much pressure for one man to handle on a day to day basis. Who was I to interrupt nature's course or the will of the universe? However, it was beneficial to be objective and weigh the ups and downs of both paths. I knew that going with the former would likely be more rewarding and would certainly help me achieve positive public recognition. "A man of action" would be a good way to be remembered if everything fell apart and I didn't make it out alive.

The swirling sphere of positive energy that was my thought process was abruptly intruded upon as an import "sports car" buzzed by me with its overrated four cylinder engine and obnoxious muffler. My irrational human impulse urged me to roll down the window and scream "you're a fucking cunt!" but I contained myself.

For one, he may have been a decent man driving his sickly mother to the hospital. And secondly, he probably wouldn't understand what I meant when I called him a cunt. I knew that the perfect word that was "cunt" had been misplaced amongst insults. Most people would assume that the word cunt was referencing an irrational and obnoxious woman.

To me, a cunt was more than that. It was a person who was intentionally doing something to draw attention to themself at the expense of another human beings peaceful state of existence. But if they were to be called out on their actions, and named as a cunt, they would immediately become defensive and claim that they were oblivious to the observation, that they were simply doing what came natural to them. That was helpful and could make one certain that said individual was in fact being a cunt because they were self-identifying.

Throughout the years some of my associates had not only committed vast and vile acts of cuntism, but had been addicted to it. Revving their engines at stoplights, blasting their stereos in front of grocery stores... and the absolute worst offense... being a middle class white male and pretending to have a ghetto accent any time African Americans were present.

My blood boiled when that offense took place. Black-men and black-women of the world were not fooled, and they were probably just as uncomfortable. I did not understand that phenomenon.

As the insect like vehicle passed and rolled off into the distance I regained my composure and began practicing the breathing exercises I had perfected in an anger management class many years before. However, I had made slight alterations to the technique. I was convinced that whoever actually developed the exercise never suffered from anger management issues. A man who was set on destruction was not thinking about breathing in through the nose and exhaling out of the mouth, he was thinking about grabbing his foe by the head and smashing his fucking face through a wall.

I vacuumed the air in with powerful, yet controlled force, deep into my lungs and held it. At that exact moment I saw a naked, beautiful blonde woman who was freshly bathed standing before me. Her body smelled excellent, like tropical flowers and high quality perfume. She floated toward me and wrapped her arms around my tense torso. I could feel her heart beating softly and her skin was incredibly smooth.

I loved beautiful, kind hearted women. If only the entire world were run by those creatures... people like me would not have needed to exist.

The vision faded and I exhaled all of the unfounded and childish hatred from my body. I did it so that I would realize what I would never have if I lashed out irrationally and found myself in jail. My violence, which was necessary, had to be carefully calculated.

The short cycle of recuperation was complete and my concentration returned. Unfortunately my five minutes of preplanning the day had been misused due to my flaws as a human. The long stretch of road ended and I made the right turn leading to the security gate that safeguarded my work place.

At the gate stood an armed guard with a neatly pressed uniform and standard issue robot smile. I respected the fact that his natural fortitude allowed him to stand there for twelve hours at a time.

I shut off the music and rolled down the window, handing my identification card to the guard. He saw that in the picture I was clean shaven and quite a few pounds lighter, and then looked back at me, his dead eyes peering through cheap sunglasses. His voice was quite serious and his question was direct. "Is that you?"

I was mildly annoyed by his lack of detective work, but replied respectfully "Yes, it is." He looked at me, and then at the identification card, and then back at me again and said "I see it in the eyes and the cheekbones now... have a good day, sir." I took the card back from him and rolled up the window as I pulled away.

I worked for a very large and powerful organization. That organization was the United States Military. I served four years active duty and that was enough. The thought of someone I had no respect for being in total and complete control of my life just didn't sit right with me. Being a civilian government employee had its annoyances, but not nearly as many as those who chose to wear the uniform.

I drove slowly, watching carefully for pedestrians who might be jogging during their fitness breaks. In between peripheral observations I turned the music back on. I had exactly two minutes until I reached my destination. It always went by much too quickly as it was the time when a song pulled you in and the final minute or so of vocal explosions was unfolding. I enjoyed it as much as I could before entering the final parking lot of the day.

I pulled into a spot far off in the corner and hid between two massive trucks. I did that for a very specific reason. I looked left, and then right, making sure no one was watching. I then tilted my head back and inspected my nostrils and teeth for debris that may have been missed during my morning cleansing.

It was imperative to do that. No one would take me seriously or be able to focus on anything I was saying if dry mucus and left over food particles were the center of attention. I took two deep breaths, shut off the engine, and exited the vehicle; grabbing the bag of energy drinks and smokeless tobacco as I did. The next phase was about to begin and my expressionless face maintained its composure as I walked through the parking lot and into the building.

Chapter 3: Conformity

Upon entering the building my nostrils were immediately overwhelmed by generic pine scented cleaning products. The underlings among my work center were instructed to use the product for mopping the floors, and more importantly, to mask the odious stink of rotting fecal matter coming from the open door of the men's restroom.

During the summer, as it was then, the foulness of a men's restroom located within a massive aircraft hangar could hardly be rivaled. It was obvious upon entry, should one dare to enter, that the restroom was intended to look nice, and to be easy to clean. The architect had done well in those two areas; however, he failed in what were the two most important aspects. There was no air conditioning, and more importantly, there was no ventilation within the restroom, the only restroom for roughly one hundred military and government employees to use.

As those observations weighed on my mind a painful cramp shot through my lower intestine. I stopped my short journey through the building, which would have ended in my workplace, and knew that I would be reporting late. The precise mixture of whisky, tobacco juice, generic energy drinks, and a decade old case of irritable bowel syndrome nearly put me on my knees. I took deep breaths, doing my best to avoid a minor panic attack, and began walking at a quick pace toward the men's restroom. With clinched teeth and heavy nasal breathing, I arrived unnoticed, and, to my delight, the restroom appeared to be empty.

Passing the urinals, I entered the first stall and closed the door behind me. Meticulously I examined the area. I knew from experience that I had less than one minute before I soiled myself. With great urgency I began the procedures necessary to defecate in that torture chamber. I saw no visible fecal matter on, or in the toilet, and no circular yellow piss stains tarnished the seat. It was a relief, but I spotted one minor discrepancy.

That particular model of toilet seat did not form a complete oval. The forward area where the penis or vagina would be closest to had been removed. I never understood that design. I did not know if that made it easier for a female to wipe herself after urinating, or if it was supposed to compensate a man with gigantic testicles. Either way, it had presented a problem that I had to deal with and I was not at all pleased about it.

In the nook there were dozens of pubic hairs of all colors, lengths, and textures. They were mangled together forming a putrid web, held tightly in place by a resin that is most commonly called dry piss. Cringing at the sight, I knew I had to press forward.

The first step was to shield myself from what I could see. Taking roughly four feet of toilet paper from the roll, I began folding it over on itself, four inches at a time. Because I had been performing that procedure for so long I was able to form a safety square within seconds. Once completed, I placed the safety square on top of the toilet's goatee and wedged it securely in place with the bottom of my boot.

Now that I was protected from the monstrosity, I continued adding layer upon layer of cheap toilet paper along every inch of the seat. The final task before I unleashed my bowels was to unravel half a roll of tissue into the pit of madness that was the toilet water. It prevented any possibility of splash back. There was no telling what kind of diseases lurked below, but I had safeguard against them.

Content with the tissue fortress I'd built; I dropped my pants and lifted my shirt, tucking it beneath my chin. Carefully I lowered myself onto the paper, making certain none of it slipped out of place. After sitting for a moment I began to relax and felt as if I was ready to relieve myself. However, nothing could ever be simple, and just when I was on the brink of relief, I heard another person enter the restroom.

My body tensed up, and beads of sweat dripped from my brow. I could hear him walk over to the urinal, unzip, clear his throat a few times, and then begin to relieve himself. I could tell that he either had a small penis or prostate problems by the faint sound that his weak stream produced as it met the bacterial sludge covering the urinal mint.

After the intruder left I was able to relax again and finish what I started.

Opening the stall door I exited cautiously, looking to my left, and to my right, relieved that the coast was clear. With haste I approached the sink and dipped my hands into the bucket of yellow, gritty, oil removing soap. I was aware that countless muck covered hands had reached into that same bucket recently, but was left without any other options to clean myself.

I read "New anti-bacterial formula!" printed on the side and it made me feel less disgusting. I scrubbed my hands together in rough and rapid fashion hoping to remove all traces of filth, down to the last bacterium fungi.

Once the rinsing cycle was complete I dried my hands with the generic brown paper towels that were dangling from the broken dispenser. The texture of the cheap and nearly useless towels was rough against the skin. Leaving the restroom, I threw the waded up bundle toward the trash can and missed it by nearly a foot. As I watched it hit the floor and tumble toward the center of the room I turned away, walking coolly as if I was an action hero and explosions were going off behind me.

I moved through the aircraft hangar quickly, but not at an alarming pace. I wanted to avoid all possible conversation and get to where I was going, yet I did not want to cause any unnecessary speculation as to why I was in such a hurry. Such things caused certain types of questions to be asked and I was in no mood to answer those types of questions. I simply wanted to get to work.

As I approached the final door within the aircraft hangar that led to my work center an imbecile that I had probably seen a thousand times, but wouldn't recognize in a police lineup looked at me as I passed and said "Hey, where's the fire?" with an obnoxious tone.

My pulse quickened at his idiotic question, and rage nearly forced my mouth to articulate the sentence "In your whore mother's pants you fucking cunt." That was clearly not advisable as I was in a place of professionalism. I chose to ignore him and enter the final door leading to the prison I would live in for the next eight and a half hours.

The door opened and I could see ten or fifteen of the guys from the morning shift scrambling around trying to get all of the tools, ongoing repairs, and general equipment turned over to the oncoming shift so they could go home for the day.

The lowest ranking guys of course had the shit jobs and could be seen sweeping up other peoples work debris and carrying out the garbage. The mid-level guys were hovering around repairs and discussing with other mid-level guys what had been done, what needed to be done, and how long they had to complete them. The highest ranking guys were standing around discussing what the mid-level and low-level guys were doing and what they would need to be doing for the rest of the shift.

As I passed each person I was greeted with a slight head nod or a thoughtless wave of the hand. There was a time, two or three years prior, that people would offer verbal greetings as I passed by. It didn't last long though. I was generally cranky and a little on edge for the first few hours of the shift and I didn't want to engage in bullshit formalities. I wanted to know what was going on, what I was expected to accomplish, and how long I had to do it. Because I had that attitude, most people avoided any verbal contact with me until after lunch time. At least that was my perception of the situation. They may have just thought that I was an asshole and not worthy of a greeting.

I approached one of the many work benches within the shop. That particular work bench had part of a wing laying on it and was surrounded by mid-level guys ready to go home. I caressed the aircraft part before me with my left hand, carefully inspecting the baseball size hole that had fully penetrated the leading edge.

Blood, guts, and feathers had exploded all over the inside of the part. Lowering my face to the hole I took a whiff of the inside to determine how fresh the kill was. It smelled like two day old putrid death and it forced me to yank my head back in disgust.

One of the guys at the bench smirked at my reaction as he spit tobacco juice into a soda bottle.

"The jet took off earlier this morning and not but two minutes later this fucking bird ran into the wing. As you can see the damage is pretty extensive... We've already had the engineers look at it and we got the tech. data right here ready to go. You guys can start the repair as soon as the shift is turned over... of course, you might want to clean the guts out of it first." I nodded at him and he grinned back at me.

I took one more look inside of the wing to really understand the full extent of the damage. I could see the bird's head, which was still attached to the remaining upper torso, twisted around backwards with some sort of gore hanging out of its mouth.

Lunch time rolled around and I was ready to leave. After unplugging my tools and brushing the hundreds of metal shavings caught in my arm hair off onto the floor, I headed for the side door exit. I wanted to avoid anyone looking for a ride or asking me to pick up food for them. I'd had all of the forced human interaction I could take for a while.

As I exited the hangar and hit the parking lot the early evening breeze cooled my skin and dried some of the sweat from my scalp. My stomach was rumbling at the thought of a hamburger and a large diet soda.

Upon entering the fast food establishment's parking lot I could see right away that they were busy. I was hoping I would be able to slide through the drive-through and then go back to my house for a few minutes, but it didn't look like that was going to be a possibility. The drive-through line was almost out into the main street, however, on a positive note, it looked like I would be able to go inside and grab the food before the rest of the second shift lunch crowd arrived, as there was no one inside.

The interior of the restaurant was decorated with turquoise, bright orange, light purple... the typical scheme that lets one know he is in the heart of poverty. I was greeted by a large, middle-aged, trashy white woman. She easily tipped the scales at over four-hundred pounds at a height of only five-foot-four. Her cheeks were flushed with blood and her skin looked clammy.

She smiled as I approached the counter. Her tooth arrangement caught my eye. The front teeth were those of a bucktoothed varmint, while the rest were of someone who had been chewing on bricks.

Her genetic code did not make sense to me and I could only guess that she was either inbred, which was not uncommon in that town, or both of her parents were over the age of fifty at her conception, which would have put her at risk for a plethora of birth defects. It was possible that she simply got fucked in the genetic roll of the dice, but I doubted it. Either way, my disgust outweighed my sympathy, and I struggled to get through the first words of the conversation without gagging.

"Hi, would you like to try one of our combo meals?"

Her voice gurgled and showed no sign of enthusiasm or professionalism. The tone was that of a prepubescent male trying to talk while squatting three hundred pounds. She stared at me with dead eyes and an open mouth… a mouth like that of a dog waiting for a treat. I was momentarily lost in her gaze and somehow the beast before me had taken control of my thoughts. Flashes of her fat, dirty body bathing in a broth of mayonnaise stole my vision. Next my sense of smell was kidnapped as she raised her arms above her head, wringing out the grease of a cheeseburger into her hair. The stink of burning rubber and boiling onions overloaded my system and I gagged, waking myself up from the temporary hypnosis.

"Sir, are you alright? You don't look so good."

My stomach turned as I looked at her but I maintained control of the situation. I breathed in deeply and replied with a hint of desperation in my voice.

"I'm sorry, I've just been out in the heat all day and I could really use a drink. Can I please have a double hamburger and a large diet soda? I won't need any fries with that." She grinned at my response, and as she did, her fat cheeks scrunched up toward her eyebrows, nearly blinding her.

"Are you sure you don't want any fries? You'll save fifty-nine cents with the combo meal. It's a win-win situation for you."

My head began spinning at the thought of her touching my food and I replied more desperately.

"Please, just keep the order as it is."

Her Shar Pei-like face formed a frown as she mumbled to herself "Well, I tried" while her sausage like fingers battered the touch screen of the cash register. I paid the beast and took my large empty cup from her massive crab claw hands.

I walked over to the fountain drink area and filled up the large cup with diet soda. I was too disgusted to take a sip of it though. The thought of anything falling off of her body, or out of her mouth and into my cup was nearly vomit inducing. I could feel a minor panic attack coming on. I was losing control of the situation. It was too much to bear, too much to think about. I started breathing heavily and my hands became moist and cramped tightly into fists.

I left the contaminated cup near the soda machine and headed straight for the exit. The behemoth behind the counter spotted me just as I reached for the germ covered handle. After a husky breath she shouted at me with her fat, gargled voice.

"Hey, Sir, you forgot your food!"

I didn't even turn around; I just kept walking out of the door and straight to my car.

After slamming the door shut I began fumbling with the keys, dropping them twice before finding the ignition and starting the vehicle. The air conditioner blasted my skin with an arctic chill and as I put the car in reverse I felt a sense of control coming back. Gripping the wheel tightly I backed out and then slammed on the gas as I put it in drive, peeling out of the parking lot with a heart full of rage and disappointment; but at least I was in control again.

Chapter 4: Lucidity

The last few weeks had been stressful at work, and since it was Friday, I'd been elected to go out with the guys for a few drinks. They had decided on a local establishment, the one right down the road from my house. The poorest, dirtiest, dumbest fucking mutants on the planet congregated at that one particular waterhole.

After quick showers and a change of clothes the guys from work and I met up out front of the establishment. All of us looked rugged and worn out, but at least we didn't smell. We all nodded our heads, and a few fist bumps and hip-hop handshakes made their way into the greeting ritual as we headed toward the entrance. I fiddled my hands around awkwardly, and did my best to fit in. Fortunately the guys were too tired to notice I had no idea what I was doing.

As we entered the building I felt like Luke Skywalker in the scene from Episode IV of Star Wars when he entered the Cantina. The smoke was so thick that all I could see were the glossy eyes and slobbery teeth of obese men and women from all walks of life, drinking, yelling, and laughing at all corners of the bar.

There was a black midget DJ who had set up his picnic table and circa nineteen-seventy record player in front of the restroom entrances. In front of him an illegal immigrant in a filthy painter's uniform danced drunkenly with a tall, skinny, and very pregnant white woman wearing daisy dukes and a cut off football jersey.

The classic sounds of Boy George's "Karma Chameleon", the hip hop version, as if anyone else in the world would know it even existed, blared loudly and the small crowd of thirty seemed to be either enjoying it, or oblivious to the fact that the entire scene was the essence of madness.

We made our way to the side of the bar where there were a few empty seats left. After taking our seats we hailed the bartender. We knew her, and she knew us. Her name was Trixie. She was sixty-something years old and used to be a Rock and Roll groupie back in her younger years.

One of the local mutants told me a few months before that she was a "fine piece of pussy" back in the late seventies. I could tell she was happy to see us as she rushed over, as I was pretty sure we were the only people who tipped her. She waved excitedly and belted out heartily to us.

"Hey! My babies are back! Let me guess? You guys want a shot of whiskey and an ice cold beer?"

We all looked at each other nodding our heads in agreement, that it was a good selection, and gave her the go-ahead on the order.

As the night went on we ordered more shots of whisky, more beers. Hours went by and we tried to have conversations here and there, but it was just too fucking loud, and too much effort. I got lost in my thoughts as I smoked a cheap cigarette I'd somehow acquired. My mind was racing back and forth between basic quantum physics, telepathy, and what Socrates true intention was by answering a question with a question. Was he just fucking with people? Or was there true wisdom in answering a question with a question, making the original question asker see the error in their original thought pattern? Jesus Christ, who really knew?

My thoughts were interrupted by what appeared to be a pale woman with short brown hair and a black hooded sweatshirt waving at me. As I stared at her, the blur began to fade and the two I just saw of her slowly became one. She looked cute from where I was sitting so I waved back with drunken confidence. She smiled and then gleefully pulled out a big piece of drawing paper from a plastic shopping bag on the barstool next to her. She began scribbling with occasional swooping motions and rapid shading. I was curious and a little terrified at the same time. Whatever was happening was not making any sense to me. Was that crazy animal drawing my silhouette? I slammed down another shot of whisky and took a hard pull from my cigarette.

About five minutes went by and then she dropped her drawing utensil, a marker I think, down on the bar. I stared at her with an open-mouth gaze, probably drooling on myself as she lifted up the large piece of paper. It was drawn just for me, but held high enough for the entire bar to witness. It was a picture of Adam, God's first man, fully naked and leaning back in a pose of ecstasy. He had a gigantic, erect cock, and spurts of semen were shooting out of the tip and all over a woman with the head of a snake. It was a very good drawing, very clear and crisp.

I didn't know what to do; I just burst into drunken laughter along with my associates and the rest of the mutants. There was little doubt that that circus freak was insane, however I just had to hear her story. I waved her over and she excitedly gathered up her drawing and a large plastic bag. As she sat down next to me I gave her a good once over, trying to contain my laughter as I did. I asked her if she wanted a drink and she responded by whispering in my ear; her voice soft and delicate.

"Yes, please. Can I have a screwdriver?"

I slurred "ssssurre" and waved down Trixie.

"Trixie, get Pecaso over here a screwdriver, make it a double!" The artist girl next to me clapped like a dolphin as Trixie sat down the drink in front of her.

The bar was getting really loud around that time. I leaned in and yelled into the crazy woman's ear sitting next to me.

"So, tell me, are you an artist or do you just like drawing big cocks in crowded bars?"

She giggled and moved closer to me so that she could whisper in my ear again.

"You looked like a nice person and I wanted to give you a present. If you let me come home with you tonight I can draw you some more big cocks."

After finishing her sentence she began to cough and opened up the neck of her sweater for relief. As she did a puff of very strong body odor seeped out, offending my nostrils, and causing my head to jerk back. The stink was sobering, at least sobering enough to know that something was very bad.

I gave my head a good shake to regain my senses after the grotesque nasal assault. Her cheeks flushed red and she grinned at me trying to hide her embarrassment. She knew I had smelled her filth. She cleared her throat and whispered.

"I haven't taken a shower in three days. My boyfriend kicked me out of his motel room down the street. If you let me take a bath at your house I promise I'll make it worth it. You can fuck me any way you want, my mouth, my ass, I don't care."

As she finished asking for the impossible I noticed what looked like track marks and small blisters on her neck. The thought of that broken animal sleeping at my house made me sick.

I leaned toward her for the last time and spoke assertively.

"Listen, I have to take a piss, I don't think this is going to work out, have a good night."

As I got up and started walking toward the black midget guarding the restroom doors, the smelly artist girl balled up the drawing of Adam with the gigantic cock and put it in my hand.

"Here, take this to remember me by, someday it will be worth millions."

I took it and put it in my pocket to avoid a possible outburst and headed for the restroom.

There was only one sink, one urinal, and one toilet in that restroom, and there were no dividers of any kind, no privacy. Feces, paper towels, vomit, and piss were all over everything. I didn't know who thought it was a good idea to shit in the urinal, but the drunken guy next to me seemed oblivious to it as he pissed on it.

As I stood in front of the toilet filled with the excrement and vomit of dozens of mutants, as I stood in the pool of urine and spit of those maniacs... A moment of clarity took me away from it all.

This truly isn't a constructive way to live my life. It would be more beneficial to spend all of my free time studying the universe, philosophy, logic... things that will help me realize my dream of becoming a truly objective thinker, a man who understands everything enough to know that he understands nothing... This is the key to true normalcy...

As I was thinking that, the black midget walked into the restroom carrying a milk crate. He dropped it down on the floor next to the paper towel dispenser, climbed on top of it, and started pissing in the sink. I was really drunk by then.

After urinating on the floor, and the wall, for fear of splashback from the rancid toilet, I walked out of the bathroom and headed back toward my stool hoping that the homeless artist had found a new home. To my relief she had. She was sitting about ten stools down from where my associates were. There were three toothless redneck mutants feeding her drinks. I thought one was a girl, but I couldn't be certain. Picasso was smiling and having a good time, and so were they. She had already forgotten about me. Problem solved.

As I headed toward my seat a thick red headed girl with average facial features, at least by drunken standards, grabbed me by the arm and asked me if I wanted to tango. I got one more shot from Trixie and hit the dance floor, which was really just a ten by ten cleared out spot on the stained carpet. As eighties pop music blasted out of the speakers I flung my arms and legs about like I was on stage at Woodstock. The reality was that I probably looked more like an unconscious senior citizen tumbling down the side of a mountain. I didn't care though. I didn't give a fuck what those animals thought. Dust in the wind.

The end of the night came to a close and my associates and I stood out in front of the bar smoking cigarettes and talking to a few of the pigs we had picked up on the dance floor. Somehow we all agreed that it was a good idea to walk back down to my house since it was so close and we were all too intoxicated to drive.

Under normal circumstances, sober circumstances, I wouldn't want anyone in my house, especially for the night. It was too risky in my other line of work; however, I was certain that I had removed all evidence of the previous execution. Well, it was more of a butchering than a simple execution.

I'd been under a great deal of stress in recent months and I needed some female companionship, even if it was with a woman I would normally consider subhuman.

We arrived at my house, but I didn't remember the journey. I pulled out a fresh bottle of whisky and poured everyone a glass to seal the deal for the rest of the night. The girls wanted to hear some music so I put my eighties rock collection on, the classic party songs that drunk girls loved to hear. As Bon Jovi rocked my living room I asked the thick redhead, I think her name was Darbie, I mumbled it to disguise my ignorance, if she wanted a tour of my house. She grabbed my cock through my pants and said "lead the way."

As we walked through the house, heading upstairs and toward my bedroom, she rubbed my arm and looked at me with her lustful eyes, the eyes I knew all too well, never from a respectable woman of course, but from a putrid whore, yes, I knew those eyes.

We got to my bedroom and I was so drunk I could hardly see. She pushed me on the bed and ripped my pants down. I started to think *I'm too far gone for this* but it was too late. She took my manhood into her mouth and brought it to life. Drunkenly I laughed at how ridiculous the situation felt and she ignored me. Once I was as hard as I was going to get, she took off all of her clothes, everything except for one of her socks. I wouldn't have even noticed except for the fact that her socks were stitched to look like giraffes from the wild kingdom of Africa. The sock went all the way up to her knee cap. I asked her why she left it on, and she replied hesitantly "I lost my toes in a lawn mower accident and I'm a little insecure about it."

I shrugged at the response and examined the animal before me. I wasn't even slightly attracted to her naked body or her stupid sock, but I was too drunk to care what happened, I was fully medicated.

She climbed on top of me and her body was extremely heavy. She bounced up and down and I could barely feel anything as far as pleasure was concerned. Mostly what I felt was pain in my hip bones. Her slamming and grinding was ruining any possible enjoyment I may have been able to derive from the encounter. I tossed her off and told her I wanted to fuck her from behind. She smiled and scrambled to her hands and knees.

I was disgusted. She was unclean. She had no attention to detail or common courtesy. The smell was similar to that of the aircraft hangar restroom. My erection started to descend as she looked back at me with wild eyes and asked stupidly "what's wrong?"

My mind searched for any acceptable answer as she stared at me. "Nothing babe, turn over on your back, I want to see your face while I fuck you."

I cringed at my own response as she flipped over on to her back.

My fortitude was fading as I did my best to please that filthy animal. Her flap jack breasts moved in a circular motion, occasionally resting in her armpits as I plunged away, working up the nerve to pretend I was cumming so I could end the madness. As I was about to tell the lie that every woman is comfortable telling, she stopped me.

"Listen, this isn't really working. You can't even get your dick hard. I think you are too drunk to even realize it... its kind of pathetic."

I pretended to look offended and pulled myself out of her body. As I looked down I realized I hadn't even been inside of her. I didn't remember at what point I was. I was relieved.

"Listen... this was kinda fun but I think I'm going to head back to my apartment. I have to work in the morning."

I looked at her with sad eyes and feigned protest.

"Aw... Darbie, I wish you could stay... How are you going to get back to your car?"

She squinted and peered at me as if I was an imbecile.

"I drove you and your friends here from the bar in my van, don't you remember?"

I was puzzled, I could have sworn we had walked, I knew we did.

"Didn't we walk here?"

She laughed loudly at my question and began writing her name and number on a piece of paper.

"Listen, if you ever want to hang out when you're not drunk, give me a call… and by the way, my name isn't Darbie, Its Francine."

We both put our clothes back on and I followed her out to make sure that she and the other idiots I brought home were gone. There was one girl and two of the guys from work half-dressed and sleeping on the couch. I really didn't want them to stay there but I could trust the guys from work to get up and leave in the morning. I was pretty sure they knew the girl somehow so she wouldn't be an issue. Besides, it looked good for me to hang out and have people over from time to time. It made me look normal.

Francine waved at me as she pulled out of the driveway and puttered away, her power steering screaming into the night as she turned at the stop sign.

After locking the door and shutting off the porch light, I checked the basement door. The two key locks and deadbolt were secure. I didn't want the people on the couch wandering down there in a drunken haze. Though I was always certain to lock it during and after use, one could never be too careful when it came to facing the death penalty if you were caught. Though all evidence that would suggest a bodily dismemberment had taken place had been chemically removed, the sound proofed walls and windows, the tools, the chemical locker, the barrels; those things would only draw suspicion. I took comfort in knowing that they would need a great deal of tooling and motivation to get past the three locks and steel plaiting that was screwed onto the other side of the door. If my friends weren't too drunk to notice the excessive locks and asked me about it later, I'd just tell them the house had been broken into when the previous tenants resided there and they had added extra locks out of paranoia. However, I seriously doubted that would be a problem.

I walked back upstairs and took off my clothes, collapsing onto the bed. Consciousness rapidly began to fade. I thought to myself... surely I wouldn't get that drunk again, at least for a while... I had work to do soon.

As I opened my eyes the familiar turning of the gut and the heavy salivating of the mouth sent me running to the bathroom. I opend the lid of the toilet and my vomit shot into the urine I didn't remember leaving behind. Maybe it was Francine's. I threw up six or seven more times. I turned on the shower and entered without waiting for the temperature to rise.

I tried to remember the previous night, but the pounding in my head was making it difficult. The story started putting itself together. I recalled the homeless smelly girl, the black midget DJ, the bathroom covered in bodily excrement, the horrible dancing... The girl who came home with me... whose genital hygiene was nonexistent. What else was there? What was I not remembering? Why did I feel so much guilt? My chin started to quiver. I collapsed in the shower sobbing like the weakling coward that I really was.

That often happened after I got too deep in the whisky, but I knew that the increased sensitivity was a chemical reaction from the alcohol and not my true feelings, as I didn't' seem to have many to pull from. I enjoyed the process of experiencing emotional pain and did not attempt to interrupt the program, even if it wasn't real. It made me feel normal.

I imagined what someone else; a regular person would feel and emulated their thought process.

I want so badly to be sober, to live by a code of honor, to make my family proud. I don't ever want to feel this way again. I don't want to be a drunkard... a sexual deviant... I have to find something to take the place of alcohol and sex. I have to find a religion... God please help me...

I scrubbed my body furiously over and over with the soapy body sponge, but it didn't wash away the filth that was in my mind that was torturing my soul. I scrubbed my skin until it was bright red and sore all over. Hot water killed bacteria so I turned the shower knob nearly all the way up and stood under the blistering heat as long as I could. The steam and the shock to my system brought on more nausea and I vomited again in the shower. There was blood in it and I knew that I had to quit drinking.

The simulated crying had become dull and I left the shower and dried off. However, the minor alcohol poisoning was real enough. I needed to rest.

Beep...Beep...Beep...Beep! I woke up sucking in a deep breath and instinctively slammed my hand down on the alarm. My eyes were crusted shut. I worked the dried bodily fluids from my lashes so I could see the time. It was seven p.m. I didn't remember setting the alarm. I felt lightheaded and lonely. My testosterone levels were starting to normalize. I could tell because my cock was rock hard and filled to the brim with piss.

As I walked into the restroom I attempted to make my cock point downwards but it was like a brick. The tip was on fire and ready to explode from the pressure. I ripped the shower curtain back and opened the flood gates. A liter of brown colored urine sprayed all over the walls, almost hitting the ceiling in the process. I eventually got it under control. As it came to a halt my cock began to burn. I didn't know if it was from the dehydration or if I'd picked up my first STD. I started to panic at the thought of having an STD, someone else's bacteria growing in my body. I was pretty sure it was from severe dehydration and mal-nutrition, but one could never be too sure. I'd chug down some water and see what happened. If it went away I would be fine. After drinking two thirty-two ounce plastic fast food cups full of water I laid back down in my bed. Only moments went by before I passed out again.

I took another long shower with extensive scrubbing and felt much better. My urine was clear like bottled water and the tip of my cock no longer burned as I pissed. That day would be the day. I would go to the grocery store and buy fresh vegetables, fruit, whole grains, lean meats, and high fiber cereals. Although I had been through the same scenario a few dozen times over the last few years, I knew I could do it that time. I could get the quality organic food products, I could start an organized exercise regimen again, and I could work my way back to a healthy lifestyle. Even if I failed, I could still tell myself that I tried. Every addict relapsed, but eventually some of them turn it around… Who was I kidding, I wouldn't last the whole day, but it would give me something to do, perhaps someone to mark.

The journey to the grocery store was uneventful. It was around eight a.m. as I pulled into the parking lot. There was a teenager out there that appeared to have some sort of Down syndrome. He looked over at me and smiled as he pushed the baskets up to the front of the store. I had thought they did that at night after closing, but apparently not. I was glad to see he had a job that was not in the actual food service industry. I remembered at one of my previous work places there was a cafeteria that was managed by two regular adults, but all of the other workers had a form of Down syndrome or retardation. It was some kind of special needs contract worked out by the state. It was very difficult to eat the food they served me. I could see spittle and drool falling from their mouths from time to time and many of them had large warts and moles on their arms and faces. I tried to be mature about the situation but the fact of the matter was that almost no one was ok with that scenario. It was just one of those situations that no one wanted to discuss because they would be *the asshole*. I'd be the asshole though... I'd admit it. No one who was drooling... no one who probably played with their asshole at random times during the day should be serving food to anyone.

As I entered the store I grabbed the cleanest basket I could see without looking like I was carefully inspecting each one, even though I really was. The grocery store was located in the heart of dirty redneck utopia. There were mutants... "Pineys" as they proudly called themselves, walking around everywhere. There was little question that almost all of them shared some sort of family ties... inbreeding. Each woman I passed was slender, but not in a healthy way. They all had the body of a starving teenage girl and the face of an old woman. Meth Amphetamine was the drug of choice out there. They all looked exactly the same other than a few of them having more teeth, or more crooked teeth than the other. They had on clothes that were probably in style during the mid-eighties. Big, filthy, white sneakers with tapered stone washed jeans and baggy neon colored shirts.

The store had a small automotive section where they did oil and tire changes. As I passed by that section looking for the breakfast food aisle, I heard a man with a terrible speech impediment yelling at the employee behind the counter. I was curious as to what was going on so I moved in closer, pretending to be looking at the ridiculous selection of hubcaps they had for sale. I was within twenty feet and could hear every word he was yelling crystal clear. He was an ugly man in his late forties, skinny as a rail. He was wearing filthy blue jean overalls and mud crusted boots. His every word was like the strum of an obnoxious banjo and created a sloshy saliva noise as it maneuvered around his twisted k-nine teeth.

"Listen here mother fucker! You aint not got no right! Do you hear me, boy?! I said YOU-AINT-NOT-GOT-NO-RIGHT! I didn't ask you to spill a drop of oil on the hood of my truck! That aint what I paid you to do you son of a bitch! I paid you my hard earned money to change my fucking oil, god dammit, and that is what you are gonna do... again! And that is all you were supposed to do the first time! But you had to go and fuck it all up! I aint paying for a god-damn-thing! You wanna spill shit on my paint job and expect me to still pay!? Fuck you! I said Fuuuuuck you! If you want me to pay, you gotta do it again mother fucker!"

It was clear that the idiot piece of shit was trying to get free service over bullshit. My child-like curiosity turned to hatred. There was nothing more in the world I wanted at that exact moment than to suplex that expendable fucking mutant straight through the concrete floor, and then proceed to urinate on his corpse. However, I would not do it there. Though the employee would likely have been grateful for my service, I would never trade jail time for my service to society.

Looking through the glass window behind the man at the counter I could see the filthy redneck's truck being serviced, again. It was a nineteen-seventy-something, rust bucket, trashcan on wheels. It was beyond laughable that he would be concerned about a few drops of oil on his hardly visible paint job... a few drops of oil that could simply be wiped off.

I tried to fathom what his childhood was like. Was it a man or a woman that taught him that behavior? Was his father closely related to his mother? Perhaps his mother was also his aunt? I could only imagine the drunken speeches he'd heard about hard work… earning respect… standing his ground. Every dumb fuck bumpkin I'd ever talked to always had a quick temper and couldn't wait to tell me about their no nonsense upbringing. Something along the lines of…

"Sheeeeit, my daddy done raised me right. We kill or get killed, we get down mother fucker!"

I'd also seen those morons get beaten half to death by a superior opponent who usually did not start the fight. And that thing about "hard work"… a few of them may have worked hard days out in the sun, but the majority of the meth-head scum bag rednecks I'd met were just petty criminals always acting as if society owed them something. They collected their welfare and their food stamps, yet gave nothing back to society for those gifts. If we lived in an ancient civilization they would be killed and possibly eaten for their lack of contribution. At best they would be slaves carrying stones toward a temple with a whip at their back and a foot in their ass.

I took down the license plate number on the old rust bucket, pretending to check messages on my cell phone as I did. When I was done I turned my basket around, the wheels squeaking and the handle shuddering, and began walking in the other direction. There was nothing for me to say or do. I was not a smooth talking counselor, I was a vigilante… If I voiced my opinion he would surely have turned his verbal assault on me, and on that day, I didn't know if I would be able to restrain myself. There was a better time and place to rid the world of him forever. I felt confident he met the criteria I required, and I would soon find out.

I decided I'd had enough of the store and its occupants. It was time to leave that place of evil. Hurriedly I grabbed the items that I came for, ignoring the useless bitch asking if I'd like a free sample, the old half blind woman asking if I knew where the mayonnaise was, the sixteen year old store employee asking me if I'd found everything ok. I ignored them all, paid for the items, and walked out the door.

Chapter 5: Apathy

Back in my kitchen it was around nine-thirty a.m. and I was starving. I hadn't eaten a thing since Friday and I was ready for a hearty man-meal. After turning on the stereo and selecting a random shuffle of sixties rock, I examined my wares. With the exception of a few pre-packaged items everything I bought at the grocery store would have been considered whole foods. I picked up a few lovely spices as well to go with the stew I'd been subconsciously plotting out since I woke up.

I saw an excellent documentary about a man who moved out to Alaska and built his own log cabin. He was a real man, a man with true grit like the cowboys in old western movies. He built that cabin from trees he'd cut down and would hunt the wild game of the region with an old beat up rifle. One particular part that I remembered, my favorite part, was when he was out hunting and came across an elk that had been half eaten by wild animals. He cut off a hind quarter and took it back to the cabin. It all took place during the deep Alaskan winter. There was snow everywhere; foot upon foot of snow… wilderness all around, no other humans for miles upon miles… and that man, that exceptional human being thrived in it.

He pulled out a large black pot and started filling it up with chopped vegetables, various spices, cubes of elk meat, and a few other ingredients. I was never a fan of stew before I saw that. When I saw him making it, that essential, hardy man-meal, I was envious. He was living day to day, surviving, making the best with what he had. He used his knowledge, no doubt passed down from an excellent teacher, and created the perfect meal.

I could just imagine looking out of that small wooden framed window in the log cabin. It was pitch-black and there were multiple feet of snow covering the ground. There was nowhere to go and there wasn't a whole lot to do. However, there was a massive pot of elk stew simmering on the stove, and its smell would bring peace and comfort to the cabin. It would remind the occupant of mother's home cooking. Yes, that was a good meal. That is what cooking should always be like; an experience. There was no doubt he slept good on that night.

I mimicked the All-American alpha male. I became him for a short time as I pushed the ingredients off of the cutting board and into the broth. Soon after, the steam rose and the first hint of certain perfection was intoxicating. I stirred in the pepper, the wisticher sauce, the sea salt, a few other spices, and finally the garlic. Everything melted together as the ladle moved back and forth through the thickening stew. It was all happening in slow motion. Jimi Hendrix played through my stereo and I could feel every string, every note.

I pulled three pounds of cubed beef from the refrigerator and massaged each piece intently, lovingly. I knew that rushing perfection only created a less than perfect product. Because I had that wisdom and I appreciated it so much I took my time with the cubes of beef. Long minutes went by as I carelessly swayed back and forth, rubbing, caressing, essentially finger fucking the cubed beef.

Jimi asked me "are you experienced?" and I replied in song "yes, I am", and as I did that I began sliding the tender cuts of beef into the pot, gently stirring as I did. Piece after piece entered and the broth steadily rose. As the final cube fell into place I inhaled through my nose, a breath of appreciation, of love and respect for that meal. I placed the clear glass lid on top of the black pot; turned the temperature down to simmer, and walked away.

I had a few hours to kill before my meal would be ready, and even though I was starving I decided to wait it out. I headed into my bedroom and sat down in front of my computer. I scanned through all of the major news websites to see what was going on in the world. I saw that politicians were still pretending to be opposed to the war, yet they were sending thousands of troops back to the Middle East to maintain the peace. We all really knew, or we were pretty fucking sure at least, that politicians and corporations were in cahoots behind closed doors and that they were making trillions of dollars by "rebuilding the Middle East". We knew that they were selfish murderers, cowards, but we did nothing about it. What could we do? The answer truly was nothing. What the fuck did I even really know about it all? As I continued browsing, an article caught my eye, "The first ladies vacation in Hawaii."

In the article the author, a female, a very, very stupid female, excitedly explained the details of the first ladies vacation. It cost over four million dollars and she had recently dined at a restaurant where each plate was over three thousand dollars. The author went on about the stylish clothing the first lady adorned, which color bathing suit she decided to wear to the beach, and how her hair looked perfect even after a tough day of nothing. That idiot author went on and on; making it seem like living the life of a leach was something to strive for. Unfortunately, a lot of western women, the type of dolts that read that type of garbage on a regular basis had princess syndrome and they simply did not understand why that fantasy life, that waste of money, was a horrible and shameful thing.

I became more and more irritated as I read on. Our nation was in a massive financial crisis yet that person, a person who was supposed to be the president's right hand, was wasting money on frivolous nonsense. What kind of example did that set? How was I supposed to believe the United States was truly that far in debt when she was blatantly showing us that we were not? Was her job really so stressful that she deserved such treatment? I highly doubted it. No one who is catered to every second of every day has a hard life, especially when that life required no physical sacrifice.

I could picture a coal miner watching the news after a fourteen hour shift in hell. His back in spasms, his cough getting worse, and he would know in the back of his mind that he could die a horrible death in that mine, maybe not tomorrow, but someday. That was true hard work. That was the kind of hard working man young American boys were taught to respect. That is the kind of person who deserved a vacation, but he'd never get one, at least not the kind that the first lady enjoyed, all on the American tax dollar.

The coal miner would continue to slave away at a job that must exist for the world to turn, for it to evolve, and he'd suck it up, because that is what he was taught to do, to be a man, a real man, the kind of man who contributed to society. And as he did, he would be belittled at best, and left out at worst, by public speakers at the nation's finest colleges. The speaker would tell the crowd that the future was in education. He would insinuate as elegantly as he could that a life without proper education was a life lost.

What he would fail to explain is that no education would be possible without the grunts of the world. The grunts, sweating and aching, who built the colleges from the ground up, who paved the parking lots, waxed the beautiful floors, served food in the cafeteria, and made the trash disappear. He would fail to elaborate on the fact that those people had to exist or there was no room for the great minds of society to deceive, to fool the masses into believing they are more important, that they were just slightly more than human. If there were no grunts to perform those jobs, the highly educated, the privileged few would not be allowed to live in such a naïve state. The pyramids would have never been built, the automobile would not have evolved into the excellent means of conveyance that it had, as there would be no grunts in the factory to mass produce the product, which in turn brought in the trillions of dollars for continued product development and research. We would not know the limits of a great mind, in the physical sense, if there were no grunts to carry out the orders of that mind. We were all in it together.

As a former college student, one without a degree, I did fully support higher education, and I respected a man with a powerful mind, I just did not understand why the world as a whole was not more objective. If I had one wish, that wish would be that everyone could clearly see and appreciate the bigger picture. A man who learned on the job, a man who attended a trade school, or a man who attended a top university… each of those men contributed in their own way. A fourteen hour shift shoveling coal is just as emotionally and physically taxing as sitting in a laboratory for fourteen hours trying to find the error in a mile long calculation. Both men would die early from wear and exhaustion chasing the American dream, that dream of what they had been taught was success.

There I went, trying to be a philosopher of some kind, pretending like I had the answers. I looked over at the clock and realized I still had a few hours before the stew would be ready. I knew that what I needed to do was go out and get some fresh air. I needed to go out and get some exercise. That day was supposed to be the day that I turned it all around. It was day one in the recovery phase, the phase that started my new and improved life. Sitting there getting angry over news articles, over the state of the world, was a waste of time. Even if I had a way to voice my frustrations, my thoughts, my remedies… no one would give a shit. I had no backing, and in this world, the world of politicians and corporations, a man without backing was a man whose words fell on deaf ears.

I changed into loose, comfortable clothing and grabbed my mp3 player as I headed out the door. There was a track near my house that the military used to exercise. It was open to the public on the weekends so I decided to head over and get in a brisk walk. As I pulled up I could see about fifty people in official military p.t. gear running around the track. It must have been a reservist weekend and they were catching up on their p.t. test. I was a little apprehensive about walking around the track while they were testing but there was no rule against it. It was open to the public, and even though I was the only civilian asshole there, I forced myself out of the car and started walking around the track.

My mp3 player had Beethoven's "Moonlight Sonata" on repeat and turned all the way up. At first it was hard for me to really get in the zone, to let my mind go, as there were men and women running by me, all of them surely annoyed by my presence, annoyed at my freedom to walk at a brisk pace instead of jogging at a brutal one.

I looked down at the ground and pretended that they were not there. Before long I felt like I was all alone, I felt at peace. I pictured myself floating through space, and as I floated a different star would light up every time Beethoven's finest work hit a new note. The stars started to look more and more like atoms, like building blocks to something much greater. Perhaps we were all just parasites, insignificant parasites crawling around on a giant atom, an atom that was one out of infinite. Yes, that was a possibility. The more I thought about it the more I liked the idea. Right then I could have been crawling around on an atom that was part of some giant god-like being. If that was the case, would I die if he died? Or would that atom just simply move on to form another type of matter? Did I even understand how atoms worked?

My meaningless thought process was interrupted by two scrawny African Americans wearing official military p.t. gear. They were about fifty feet in front of me. A skinny young man was holding a skinny young woman in his arms and was trying to carry her off of the track and into the grass. He was having trouble though as he was too weak to support her weight. As I got closer I took off my headphones to better analyze the situation. I could see that the girl was hyperventilating and tears were running down her cheeks.

I asked the young man carrying the girl what was happening, and if I could help. I was ignored completely as he stumbled past me. A large, black, professional looking man with a cell phone, a whistle, and a clipboard ran up to the couple that had crumbled together in the grass, his female aide following right behind him. The large man kneeled down to examine the girl. I asked again if there was anything I could do and all four of them, even the hyperventilating girl stopped and stared at me for a moment, and then went back to ignoring me.

The large professional man came to the conclusion that she was either having an asthma attack, a heart attack, or a panic attack. He called for an ambulance. As he did the hyperventilating girl started flailing her arms about. I could see that they did not require my help as they were hardly even acknowledging my existence. I put my headphones back on and listened to Moonlight Sonata as the young girl writhed around on the ground before me. I was not sure what to do so I just stood there and stared at her.

A few minutes passed by and the girl seemed to be calming down. I determined that her life was not at risk and that my presence in no way could help her even if she was in mortal danger. I turned around and walked back onto the track to finish my workout, to finish my thoughts about being a useless parasite. As I did it occurred to me that the reason they may have been ignoring me was my apparel. I looked down and remembered that I was wearing a little-too-tight turquoise, cartoon covered Christmas t-shirt, cargo shorts, and black socks. I supposed to someone in the military it would have appeared that I didn't have the answers for such a potentially serious problem. I shrugged it off and headed back home to check on my stew.

Chapter 6: Throes

The internet was a wonderful thing. In only three hours I'd discovered... simply starting with a license plate number, that my next project, Jebediah Winston Tarner, the disgusting snake toothed redneck from the grocery store, was not only a two time sex offender, he was currently wanted for failure to appear in court and being delinquent on child support payments. He had been arrested seven times in the previous twenty-nine years for crimes ranging from burglary to sexually assaulting both a woman, and a minor. The more I dug up, the more hatred I had for that waste of life. He would suffer greatly for his crimes against humanity... women... children. I would take pleasure in ripping him apart...

The stew let me know that it was done. The amazing aroma of fresh vegetables, a dozen spices, and three pounds of beef filled every cubic foot of the house. My nose was in heaven as I followed the scent out of my room, down the stairs, and into the kitchen. I looked through the cabinets and found the biggest bowl in my shitty bachelor inventory. It looked like it could hold at least a gallon. Even though I was supposed to start eating correctly on that day, meaning correct portions as well, I simply couldn't resist filling the bowl to the brim.

I removed the clear glass lid from the pot and ecstasy washed over me as the rolls of fantastically flavorful steam took over every sense within my body. I could feel the comforting warmth on my face; I could hear the hardly present hum of water boiling... just ever so slightly. I could taste the fumes all the way from the tip of my tongue to the deepest depths of my lungs, and I could see with full clarity the beautiful stew before me. The wonderful colors of the vegetables, the luscious, oily glaze of the broth, the thick, hearty chunks of meat floating on the surface... If it hadn't been boiling hot I would have scooped it out with my hands and rubbed it all over my body. I would have stripped down to nothing and masturbated with the oily surface residue as I ate the hardier portions of the stew. That was how excellent it was. That is how hungry I was. That was the power of a properly cooked meal. That was an experience. That was what a wolf in the wild would feel after starving for days... and then finally he sees an innocent little bunny rabbit and rips his body apart without mercy. He would do it to survive, and as he did it he would taste the fresh blood, the nourishment, and it would taste amazing. That is what he was born to do. That is what I was born to do. I would devour, I would savor every moment, and I would become the wolf.

After I finished pouring the stew into the massive bowl I saw that there were no clean spoons left in the drawer. The ladle was lying on the stove, the ladle that helped make all of it possible. I would use that. A spoon would not have sufficed for a meal such as the one I had created. I had the food of a barbarian, the food of a Viking God. I filled up the ladle and gently blew the steam away from the solid portion. After a few moments I knew it had cooled enough for consumption and slowly emptied the ladle into my mouth. The taste... the flavor, the majesty of it all was overwhelming. I could feel the warmth throughout my entire body. As the bowl of stew conformed to room temperature I shoveled it faster and faster into my mouth.

As I sat there in a fake leather chair with a bottle of whiskey and a gut full of beef stew... as I sat there listening to the soulful sounds of Aretha Franklin, Phil Collins, and Stevie Ray Vaughan... My mind wandered from one place to another. I analyzed myself. Why was it that I loved whisky so much? Was it subtle training from childhood? Did I hear that whisky was a hard man's drink? Did I ever think I would become a real man like John Wayne for taking it straight from the bottle, followed by no grimace or sign of displeasure, just an expressionless face, a face formed by a decade of discontent?

I couldn't recall the first time I had whisky, or the first time I was whisky drunk, but one thing I could recall was that it had always been my favorite way to release. Every time I drank whisky I was somehow forced to face my fears, things I had tried to hide from myself deep within my subconscious.

As the angelic voice of Aretha screamed into my ears *Freedom…Freedom….Freedom!* I lit a cigarette, took another swig from the brown bottle, nodded my head in appreciation, and broke down that final door. That door that didn't want the real shit to come out. The shit I did not want to face.

A memory of pain flashed before me. I was standing in front of a class of pharmacology students and there was nowhere to hide. I was exposed. It was my turn to give a seven minute speech, a topic that covered the power of drug addiction, the process of the brain when it received its dosage, and how one could overcome the need of that drug.

I was handsome, well-muscled, dressed from head to toe in clothes I couldn't afford, and ready to blow their minds. I held the notes I typed up the night before to chest level. I waited for the class to become quiet, so quiet that you could truly hear a pin drop; when it was to that level I knew I was ready, it was show time.

At that time my physical presence commanded attention. My deep voice filled with raw emotion, conviction, and confidence began saying the words I had rehearsed for hours the week prior. As each word passed my lips my confidence increased. I made eye contact with various students in the room, and as I did I began to walk back and forth. I pointed my finger here, waved a hand there, and balled my fist to show my passion for the subject as I reached critical points. As I went on I could see the females in the room follow me with their eyes. I had their attention; I had their respect and their admiration. I was a good looking man with a clear message and I didn't give a shit what anyone else thought. For that brief moment, I had them. After a few minutes my brain went on cruise control. I let it ride and it felt good. I was the man for a moment.

As I continued I started noticing that some guy in the small classroom audience was playing with his calculator... and a girl in the background was reading a novel... and another guy was sleeping. My eyes began to dart back and forth as the words started to stumble, as they started to fall apart. I realized that I was full of shit, and everyone knew it. As each second passed I saw more and more people looking out of the window, checking their cell phone messages... the teacher was looking down at his grade book. I crumbled. I wasn't a strong, handsome man with a powerful message. I wasn't any of the things I pretended to be. I instantly became self-aware. I was just another nineteen year old asshole giving a speech that no one gave a shit about, not even my teacher. My throat swelled shut and sweat exploded from my body. I couldn't feel my feet anymore and I felt like I was on the verge of having a mental breakdown. I wanted to disappear and erase that moment forever. I froze.

I wanted attention, and I got it after I stopped talking halfway through my speech. Ten, twenty, thirty seconds went by. Everyone was locked in. I could sense their discomfort, their hope that I would just wrap it up and sit down. I panicked. I said to them all

"I apologize for this interruption, my asthma is setting in and I'm having difficulty breathing."

With that statement I left the room and didn't come back until my next class which was two days later.

That was a powerful moment for me. That was the moment that I realized it didn't matter how many weights I lifted, how many expensive clothes I wore, or how proud I stood; I couldn't fake confidence, I couldn't fake personality, I couldn't fake being what I perceived to be a real man. I was living a lie. I was an insecure child living in a man's body. I had failed at being normal.

I got chills just thinking about it, and not the good kind, like the kind you get when you hear Stevie Ray Vaughn play his rendition of "Little Wing". No, they were the kind of chills that kept you up at night, the kind that made you humble yourself. However, on a positive note, I wouldn't have traded that moment for anything. That was the moment that started my path toward total honesty, complete integrity. From that day forward I knew that no matter how important I thought I was, there would always be that potential to falter in the face of adversity. There would always be the possibility that it could happen again.

I took another swig of whisky and put on Dusty Springfield's "Son of a preacher man". It wasn't the time to get philosophical, or to get lost in one memory. No, it was time to let loose. It was time to face my fears; it was time to release those dormant demons. I tapped my foot and took a hard pull from the cheap cigarette I shouldn't have been smoking in my house. God damn it tasted good. After a few more hard pulls on the butt, I knew that it was time to face another obstacle; it was time to relive another memory.

When I was thirteen years old my foster parents sent me to a psychiatric hospital that housed both children and adults. My ever increasing apathy and disregard for authority... The dissection of my pet, those things had finally worried my foster parents enough to seek professional help.

Early on at the age of five years old I remembered vividly the first time I became aware that adults were just as fallible as children. I was in a daycare center after kindergarten until my mother would get off of work. The woman who would watch over the children was a church going, goofy-sweater-wearing, evil witch.

When the parents would drop off the children she would put on her kind eyes and gentle smile. Once we were alone with that demon of a woman she would torment us with her cruelty. At the time I felt a deep connection with my foster mother. I never wanted to leave her side and I would cry every day when she would walk out of the daycare door. The witch would pretend to console me and then walk me back to where the other children were playing.

She warned me to be quiet, to stop crying, but it never worked. Her temper was fierce and would quickly become tired and annoyed with my whimpering and take me into her office where she would proceed to whip my backside with a thin wooden paddle which brought on more tears and more whimpering. I remember her standing over me, her red painted finger nail pointing directly at my face. The witch would demand that I stopped acting like a baby at once. I was so afraid at that time.

After a few weeks of that I started refusing to get in the car with my mother to go to daycare. I would sit on the ground and bury my head in my knees, forcing my mother to pick me up and sit me in the car. She would ask me why I didn't want to go. I only responded with silence. It didn't take her long to realize that something wasn't right.

She dropped me off as usual and then waited out in the parking lot for a while before re-entering the daycare facility. Fortunately for me, I was being whipped by the demon witch as my mother came walking into the office. I don't remember exactly what she said, but she screamed and attacked the demon, slapping and punching her all over the head and pulling her hair very hard, jerking her to the ground. After that day, I never had to go to daycare again.

That was the beginning for me. I was still very young, but began to understand that adults were not all good, they were not in total control, they didn't have all of the answers, and I was never going to be completely safe. From that day on I had no respect for any adults other than my parents, I would simply ignore them.

My apathy began to develop a few years later and reached its peak around the age of thirteen. I recalled my father running over the dog he had gotten me for my birthday just a few months earlier. He was still a little puppy, a black lab named Tommy. I did find entertainment in watching him run around, but was unable to form a bond with the creature.

One Saturday morning my father was late for work and ran out of the front door, hopping into his car quickly and wasting no time pulling out of the driveway. Naturally, the puppy followed the running man, but my father paid no mind to him. As he sped down the driveway in reverse the curious and excited puppy got caught up beneath the front left tire and was killed instantly.

My father slammed on the brakes after realizing what he had done and got out of the car. As I approached him, and my fallen companion, I could see a great sense of shame and remorse in my father's face. I stared at him, and then at the puppy, expressionless. He tried to console me but, no consoling was required. I just replied "OK" to all of his gentle talk, all while keeping my eyes on the puppies ripped open abdominal area. His innards hung out and I was fascinated with them. I had never known what was inside of an animal, what was inside of me.

My father left for work and my mother helped me bury the puppy in the backyard and she said a prayer for him. Afterward she gave me a hug and told me to go and play, that my puppy was in a better place. I nodded and hugged her back so that she would go away. I waited a few minutes, knowing she would be caught up in her sewing before long.

After pulling the puppy from the dirt I went to the side of the house where the water hose was and rinsed all of the dirt from his fur, and his open wound. Next, I carefully snuck him away into the nearby woods where I would study his anatomy.

I didn't have much of an idea as to what I was actually doing or looking for, I just felt a great deal of excitement, something so rare I still cannot recall knowing that feeling before that time. I laid Tommy on a tree stump, his belly facing me. I looked around in every direction, paranoid that someone would interrupt my new experiment. I was far enough away that no houses could be seen, and I could hardly hear any other children playing. Most of them were too afraid to come back into the woods anyway.

Taking the tiny pocket knife my father had bought me for boy scouts, I began to slice Tommy's skin, further opening the wound on his belly. I then moved his intestines around with the blade, only having a vague idea as to what I was looking at. I had only seen the very basic cartoon anatomy pictures they show to children in elementary school. The smell of his open wound was not pleasing, nor was it too much to bear. It was just new. Seeing his insides... smelling them... it made me feel vulnerable. I could just as easily end up in Tommy's situation if I was not very careful each day.

As I was cutting away one of his hind legs to get a better look at how it worked on the inside I was startled by a young man's voice. It was Richard, a boy around thirteen years old who lived down the street. He knew me, and would bully me a little from time to time, but nothing out of the ordinary. "Hey Sullivan, what the hell are you doing back here?"

I was frozen, unsure of what to do. I knew if I was caught dissecting the animal I would probably be in trouble. I had no answer for the intruder and decided to just stand there, staring down at my work, hoping he would disappear. I was not so lucky. Richard came from behind and looked over my shoulder. He sounded as if he was about to say something, but as he peeked over he saw the blood on my hands, the pocket knife, and the butchered little puppy, Tommy.

He screamed, backing away slowly before turning and sprinting away toward the neighborhood only a hundred yards away. A small sense of satisfaction came over me before realizing I needed to get rid of the little body. I carried Tommy away from the stump and looked for somewhere to hide him. My options were limited, as the ground was flat and there weren't many leaves lying around. I decided to bury him behind a large tree.

Hastily I dug into the earth with my left hand, and cut away at it with the knife in my right. The faster I dug, the more my fingernails began to peel upwards, and small cuts opened up along the tops of my hands from the tree roots defending the hole I was trying to dig. It wasn't but two or three minutes later, after Richard had run away screaming, that I could hear his father and my mother calling out my name and heading in my direction.

I ripped at the roots, and pulled at the earth, but I could not get deep enough to conceal the body. Their footsteps were nearer, and their voices louder with each second that past. I gave up. There was no way I would be able to explain myself, or justify what I was doing. I just sat there on my knees, Tommy lying in front of me, waiting for the adults to come and find me.

"John… what the hell are you doing? What is this?" Richard's father peered down at me in bewilderment, his hands held in front of him as if he was holding up the air. My mother gasped and placed her hands over her mouth, her wide eyes staring at me, and then at Tommy. Richards's father instructed me to put down the knife, and as I did he picked it up and threw it into the woods. My mother told me to come to her and she inspected my expressionless face, my empty eyes, and then my hands. She started crying after seeing my torn up fingernails and Tommy's blood covering my palms and forearms.

That was the last time I was ever caught with an experiment. The following weekend I was placed in a psychiatric facility for sixty days. My parents came by every Tuesday and Saturday to sit in on a counseling session with the other children and their parents, and then we would spend one hour together for family time.

During the counseling sessions I was quiet in the beginning, but soon discovered that if I played nice and pretended to be interested it would be possible for an early release. I became more talkative in each session and feigned happiness from time to time. I would smile at my parents when they entered the counseling room, something I hadn't done for quite some time. They considered it a relief, progress, a sign of hope.

When my parents weren't around, the staff was surprisingly caring and professional. I was wary the first few days of my stay, but soon dismissed them, as they showed no signs of being a threat to me.

I met a lot of other children during my stay, but they were not like me. Some had mild forms of mental retardation; others had facial or other bodily disfigurements that caused them to lash out at the cruel children who would make fun of them. Others were sent in by the state, taken from their birth parents due to severe neglect. They would stay there for a while before being put in a foster home. The only child I remembered specifically, though, was a girl around my age, fourteen or so, who refused to speak. Her name was Gloria... Gloria something... She had long brown hair parted down the middle and always wore a sweater and blue jeans. I remember thinking she was pretty. I liked her. I had never liked a girl before and the feelings were unusual. They felt warm and comforting, something I hadn't had much experience with.

After four weeks of going back and forth to the schooling they offered, to the dining facility, and of course to the counseling sessions, it all just became a mindless routine. If we behaved well and participated in the classroom, and in therapy, we would receive little plastic tokens that were worth five points each. If you collected enough of them you would be able to purchase comic books, children's chapter books, and even ice cream. There was a large locked closet near the lounge area where we were allowed to sit and play for the last two hours of the day, and inside is where all of these items were kept.

I had finally gained enough tokens to purchase something from the store. I wasn't sure what I wanted, as there were not many things that interested me at the time. After the nurse opened the door she escorted me into the big closet and I looked all around the room trying to decide on something. A few minutes passed and the nurse became impatient, as I had not even asked about an item yet. She was still polite in her words, but I could sense the annoyance in her tone. "John, sweetie, I need you to go ahead and pick something out now, ok?"

I nodded at her and reached for a book. The front cover read "Robin Hood". I brought it back to the lounge area and the girl, who never spoke, Gloria, came and sat next to me to see what I had. I showed her the cover, and then handed it to her. I wasn't going to read it. She smiled and took the book from me and walked over to the corner where she had been sitting and began flipping through the pages. Her expression was relaxed, peaceful, for the first time since I had known her.

Around twenty or thirty minutes later the nurse came from behind the desk and was doing a mandatory check. Looking behind the couches, inspecting us for signs of self-harm or bullying from other children, asking us how we were feeling. As she approached Gloria she saw that the book I had bought earlier was now in her possession. The nurse leaned down, placing her hand on the book and saying Gloria's name to get her attention.

"You haven't earned any tokens since you've been here; you are not allowed to use anything from the closet until you start behaving appropriately." And with that she ripped the book from Gloria's hands and started walking toward me to return it. Gloria's face turned dark, as dark as any I've seen to this day. Her breaths were heavy and her eyes slanted downward. She stood up, tears falling from her cheeks, and ran after the nurse. The nurse turned around at the sound of little footsteps stomping nearer, and as she did, Gloria's hands shot up her white skirt, the uniform that all the nurses wore, and began ripping and tearing away at the woman's private area. The nurse howled in pain and called out for help. Two male nurses in white uniforms came running out of the door next to where the woman had been sitting and grabbed Gloria by the arms and waste, commanding her to let go.

Gloria refused. She screamed loudly, breaking her long silence and calling the woman a whore and a cunt as she yanked harder and harder. The woman nurse, crying, begged the male nurses to get Gloria away from her. They did not want to touch the private area of the woman so they grabbed Gloria's little arms and squeezed them tightly, ripping them backwards. As they did, her tiny hands became visible again. They were balled up into fists and globs of pubic hair stuck out from in-between her knuckles. She spit in the faces of the male nurses and told them they were going to die.

I remember being in awe of her, seeing the psychological power she had over the big, strong adults. From that day on, the nurses treaded lightly when dealing with Gloria. They still performed their duties, but with much more respect and patience. I don't remember anyone ever trying to take something from her again.

Though there were many incidents that took place in the hospital that caused a range of emotions, from rage to depression, to intrigue, the single most infuriating moment took place when I was going to have my supposed final psychological evaluation. It would determine whether or not I would be able to leave the hospital and spend the Christmas holiday with my parents.

I walked into the room where a bearded man stood. He was wearing the kind of clothes a college professor might. Brown leather shoes, dress pants, a turtleneck cotton shirt, and a sweater vest. He held a clipboard filled with papers in one hand and an expensive looking pen in the other. His long brown hair was peppered with grey and combed neatly. His glasses rested on his large, red nose, and were thick with a black plastic frame. He told me to have a seat and began asking me questions. His tone was that of an adult who was being insincere, but was trying to hide it.

"Good morning John, I've just spoken to your other counselors and they feel that you are, well... making some progress, but with a few hang-ups. I'd like to go over some things with you and see if we can tap into these private issues... would that be alright?"

I didn't answer him. I just nodded as I watched the clipboard in his lap.

"Now... John, you haven't been in much trouble here, and you are doing quite well with your school work, but there is something we are concerned about... You seem to not have any strong emotional responses regardless of the stimulation. It appears to us that you might be hiding your feelings deep inside... that you are telling us what we want to hear and not what we need to know in order to better help you..."

As he droned on and on with psychological terms that I did not understand at the time, deep rooted feelings of anger began to make my blood boil. I thought I had them fooled, but they had the advantage, they were adults and they had seen children like me before. My fake smiles, my forced answers in the classroom... they knew.

It was the first time I recall that feeling, that loss of control... a deep desire to punish. I was only thirteen but I could tell by his tone that he was not going to sign the papers to let me leave, to see my family for the Christmas holidays.

I looked out the window at the beautiful trees and away from the man, trying to hide the tears of fury that were resting on my eye lashes. He asked me a few more questions but I didn't want to look at him, or to answer him. He sighed and his new tone of voice is what I would recognize now as a sign of predatory behavior. It was soft, but with a hint of wickedness lurking in its midst.

He instructed me to sit next to him on the couch, putting his hand on my knee as I did. I became very uncomfortable as he massaged my flesh and spoke quietly into my ear.

"We feel like it may be beneficial for you to stay here for a few more weeks so that we can run more tests. We really want to know what is going on inside of you so that we can help you better acclimate to society when you leave here. You want to be normal don't you? You don't want kids running away from you every time you come around."

He then took his hand from my knee and put it around my shoulder, hugging me close to his breast. His breath smelled of cigarettes and mints as he went on.

"If you can just open up a little here today, I can help you... what do you say, John? Would you like to talk to me about anything... private?"

At the time I wasn't sure what his intentions were and the rage... the thought of not going home when I was told I would... I was unable to control myself. As he continued his creepy dialogue of bullshit I saw that the expensive looking pen was lying down on the clipboard he had set on the table in front of us.

His chin rested on top of my head and he began to ask me more personal questions, questions about my body, my genitals... I knew that was wrong, and I hated him for what he was doing. The embarrassment, the shame, the lies... I had to hurt him like Gloria had hurt the bitch nurse. He would learn to fear me... that I was in control.

Quickly and decisively I jerked away from him, grabbing the pen and thrusting it over and over into the flesh of his thighs. He squealed and pushed me away, sending me tumbling to the floor. He then ran to the wall by the door and frantically pushed the orange emergency button below the intercom to send in the nurses. Picking myself up from the floor I ran back toward him and began stabbing him in the back and cursing him with every dirty word I knew as he screamed for help. He turned and grabbed me by the throat, slamming me onto the carpet and restraining the arm that had been jamming the pen into his body.

The next few hours were a haze, as the counselor who had evaluated me had punched me in the head multiple times in order to stop my assault. The next memory that I recall is lying in a hospital bed. My foster parents, a doctor, and a police officer were standing in the room with me. My mother asked me how I was doing, and tried to comfort me, though I didn't feel much of anything. My father paced back and forth angrily, stopping from time to time and pointing in the police officers face, which eventually caused him to be escorted out of the room and into the hallway so that they could further discuss the incident.

The next day, my parents took me home and did their best to make me feel welcome and safe. I had ice cream every night after dinner, and the television, though I didn't find much pleasure in watching it, was mine. The only shows I enjoyed where the same ones my mother loved to watch, the old re-runs of James Dean movies and his TV show. Mr. Dean became what I wished I could be. Women swooned over him, men respected him, and he always had something cool to say regardless of the situation. He was likeable, he was normal, he fit in. No one watched him with suspicion or resentment in their heart.

My parents told me that the doctor who had assaulted me was found guilty of sexual assault and battery, among many of the other charges, after my statement inspired other children to come forth and testify... most of their stories much more horrifying than my own. He lost his license to practice and was sent to prison. He was due for release soon, only ten months from then, and I would be waiting for him when he got out.

Aside from that, the psychiatric hospital wasn't all horrible, but I did have a sense of abandonment from my foster parents. Looking back on it, now that I am older, I realize how my behavior would have looked to a normal human being. What my parents did was necessary. Had I not been placed in the hospital after dissecting my puppy, Tommy, I may have never learned to pay attention to every detail, to be very careful… to never get caught doing something abnormal again. As for the doctor… Objectively speaking, I am thankful that he showed me just how evil human beings could be. I often fantasize about cutting away his flesh and feeding it to him raw, forcing him to swallow it and choke on his own vomit… Soon.

Ah, memories. I'd brought myself into that dark place again… it was that god damn whisky. I'd be alright the next day, I just needed to rest.

Chapter 7: Evoke

It was dark; I think it was around eleven p.m. The road ahead was wet from the evening drizzle and the reflection of the moldy, yellowish street lights made the pavement sparkle like broken glass. I was drunk as hell but I needed to get out of the house. Although the sidewalk was roughly two feet to my left I did not want to walk on it unless I saw headlights. The thought of low hanging, unkempt branches making contact with my face irritated me. I couldn't stand it when something touched my face that wasn't supposed to.

I knew that I was taking a risk by being intoxicated in public, but I hadn't seen the police drive down that road, ever. Even if a cop was to find me out there, intoxicated, I would have just told him I was walking home from the bar. I seriously doubted he would press the issue any further, as it was not uncommon to see people out late at night in that pathetic excuse for a town. That is just the way it was around there.

My tennis shoes were absorbing the water from the potholes I kept stepping in. The cool, dirty, oily water felt good in the humid summer heat. I was surprised that it was so quiet outside. I heard no dogs barking, no cars off in the distance, no drunken mutants jabbering on their porch, no insects rubbing their legs together. It was just silent; silent except for my drunken feet dragging across the pavement and my nostrils pushing out air like a bull ready to charge.

I pulled out a cheap, wrinkled, half broken cigarette from my pocket and sparked up. The sudden rush of nicotine made me lightheaded and nauseous, but I'd been down that road before. It would pass, I just needed to keep smoking and not think too much about it. I took heavy pull after heavy pull and realized I was smoking the filter. I flicked it toward some sad fucks house and lit up another, and then another. I didn't know how much time had passed since I'd left my home, hell; I didn't even know where I was going. I just wanted to keep walking and keep smoking.

"Hey there... yeah you, you silly mother fucker!" The cackling sound of a female voice that's smoked one too many packs of cigarettes called to me from the tailgate of a truck just ahead of where I was. As I approached I saw that she had blonde hair and was in her late forties. She was wearing a faded t-shirt with some shitty beer company logo on the front pocket, tight blue spandex shorts, and leather sandals that were so crusty they looked to have been robbed from the grave of Jesus Christ himself. I recognized her face from the bar, but I couldn't remember her name. I knew I'd spoken to her multiple times in a drunken stupor. I recalled her being harmless... *Fuck it* I thought; I'd see what she wanted.

"Hey sweetie, can I bum a smoke from you?"

I stopped in front of her and looked her up and down. Her shirt was tied in a knot off to the side of her midsection. I could see dark red and purple stretch marks all across her abdomen. I'd always considered those war wounds that only a husband should see, as he was the only one who would appreciate their meaning. I was disgusted by her lack of style, but was too intoxicated to make a fuss about it. I reached down into my pocket and pulled out a twisted soft pack of cigarettes. The cigarette that I pulled out was the last one. I crumbled the pack as I took it out so that she could see I really had no more.

"Sorry babe, this is my last one, and it is just one of those crazy nights where I really want it for myself."

She made a pouty face, the fakest one I'd ever seen. In the voice of an old gross witch trying to pretend to be a needy child she said "Come on, baby. I haven't had a cigarette all day and I've been stuck here for hours waiting for my stupid-ass brother to get back. Help me out here." I took her plea into consideration.

The truth of the matter was that I felt sick from all of the chain smoking and walking in the humidity. I really didn't want it. But, I'd fuck with her a little bit. I felt so strange right then. It was like I was on a different wave length than the rest of the universe. I'd toy with her a bit and see what came of it.

"I'll tell you what, sweetheart... come in close so I can whisper it in your ear."

She did as I requested, and as she did I could smell her hair, her skin; she smelt like sweat and camp fire smoke. My tone was as soft as an angel's as I drunkenly whispered into her filthy ear

"If you suck my cock, right here, right now, I'll give you this last cigarette... hell, I'll even light it for you."

She playfully slapped my wrist and pulled away, pretending to protest.

"Come on baby, just let me have it, it has really been a long day."

I chuckled at her response. I knew she wanted to suck my cock. The filthiness of it was in her nature. She was one of them, a broken animal. I looked her deep in the eyes and said it one more time.

"If you want this cigarette, you are going to have to earn it. It is up to you..."

The nearly fifty redneck woman with the devilish grin on her ugly face pushed me back onto the tailgate and unzipped my cargo shorts. She pulled my underwear out of the way and started jerking me off in an attempt to get me hard. Before going any further she stopped and spoke.

"You know... if I didn't know you I wouldn't do this... I don't do this kind of thing for everybody, but Trixie always says how nice you are... So I guess tonight is your lucky night... John Sullivan. But after this, don't be such a tease when I see you down at the bar, got it?"

I laid all the way back and closed my eyes expecting her mouth to feel like sand paper. I couldn't have been more wrong. Her mouth was warm, silky smooth, and she knew how to use her tongue. I was barely maintaining consciousness but she managed to get me all the way up. Only three or four minutes passed by and I was ready to cum. Normally, I would warn a woman, at least a woman that I had some sort of respect for. I didn't respect her. I couldn't even remember her name. I didn't give a shit.

As she sucked harder and harder I could feel my balls tighten up and my ass cheeks clinch together. I shot my load deep into her throat. To my surprise she didn't pull away. She kept sucking until I was fully cleaned out. As relaxed as can be I lifted my head up to look at her as she took her mouth away from my cock. She spit my load off into the grass and wiped her chin with the back of her hand.

"Alright then motherfucker; that'll be one cigarette, thank you very much!"

With no expression and no resistance I slowly sat up and handed the dirty old hag my last cheap, crinkled up cigarette, and as promised pulled out my lighter, but the witch waved my hand away. She reached down into her ugly, faded shirt, and pulled out a pack of soggy, sweat-soaked looking matches from her bra. I looked at her, perplexed. She noticed my confusion and said "I like the way the sulfur tastes with the tobacco."

The first four were water logged and wouldn't spark, but she was determined and the fifth match lit the beat up stogy. As the match ignited, her face was illuminated and I could see her with full clarity. Discomfort and shame clawed at what little conscious I had, but I ignored it, the feelings would pass. That wasn't the first time I'd had a sexual encounter with a dirty woman.

As she sat next to me smoking and jabbering on and on about how much of a piece of shit her brother was, and how a big check was coming her way from a dead relative, the nausea took over. I tried to hold it in as I stared at her black tooth-filled mouth going up and down. I simply couldn't contain it and I was too dizzy to move. The vomit bursted out, covering her shirt, and her crinkled and marred belly. She slapped me across the face and pushed me off the side of the tailgate. As I rested on my knees, more whisky and stew spewed out into the grass. After a few minutes I felt much better, and the nagging voice of the witch faded back in. She was trying not to yell, as it was late at night, but she wasn't doing a very good job. I stood up and started walking away, back towards my house, ignoring her insults and giving her the middle finger.

When I got home I collapsed on my bedroom carpet. The vomiting had sobered me up but I still felt weak and dizzy. I'd wait there a while and then try to take down some water. I began to wonder if the old pig that had just given me oral pleasure would call me out on it the next time I saw her at the bar. I supposed it wouldn't cause me any problems, I'd just deny it if any of my coworkers were present. They knew how crazy the people were around there. Fuck it, I didn't even care. I closed my eyes and before long my mind drifted toward the thoughts I had been putting off for a while, my purpose, my reason...

Over the last twelve years I'd committed acts which society, if they were aware of them, would deem as vile, and even unspeakable. Woman beaters, rapist, child predators, murderers… I had slaughtered them all. I did receive a sense of satisfaction during, and upon completion, however, something was still missing; a companion. I'd put it off constantly but perhaps it was time for me to start taking care of myself a little better. It was time for me to seek out a beautiful woman, a clean, sober, intelligent woman.

The problem was that I didn't know if I would be able to hide my true nature from her. I'd only had one serious relationship with a female before, twelve years before, my last year in high school, and it was easier then. I was only dissecting animals, not humans, and I was still in my infancy at that time. It wasn't a major distraction to me; it wasn't a fully encompassing passion, a thing that I had to do. Ah… My first love…

We had just moved a few towns over after my father had received a promotion to regional manager at his software company. The move made it easier for him to travel to the majority of the business offices he was responsible for, and it gave me a new start. Even though it had been four years since I was caught dissecting my puppy, Tommy, no one had forgotten about it, and none of the girls at my previous school wanted anything to do with me.

The girl that I came to have interest in was lovely. Her name was Sophia. She had a beautiful face, long blonde hair, a young and firm body, and was clean and wholesome. She was so innocent. I met her at a movie theater where we both worked on the weekends. Every Friday and Saturday night we would stand next to each other in the front booth and hand out tickets to the customers coming in to see the newest films. Once the lines died down we would have time to talk in-between the late night stragglers. I had not had many conversations with females, well, other than my foster mother, so I wasn't sure how to communicate with her. She thought I was shy and told me it was cute.

Over time I began to develop feelings for her. We would go out and get fast food after school, and as we sat, enjoying our hamburgers, she would tell me about what she was going to do after high school, and what colleges she was thinking about attending. I didn't say much but she didn't seem to mind. She liked talking to me. I was a good listener and was able to offer more mature conversation than the other boys at our school.

One night after work my father had let me borrow his car and I ended up giving her a ride home. We sat in front of her parents' house for a long time and she wanted me to stay there for a while so that we could talk.

As the conversation went on she took my hand in hers and started crying. She told me how much she was going to miss me when she went off to college. I squeezed her hand to comfort her and as I did she leaned in and kissed me. Her lips tasted sweet and a rush of passion washed over me. We sat there for the next two hours just holding each other. It was a wonderful moment for me. She made me feel alive, and that some things in life did matter. Every day after that night, for months, we spent all of our free time together. It didn't matter what we were doing, we were side by side, hugging, kissing, and trying to make each other laugh. It felt incredible.

I remember her funeral well. Everyone was crying and my mom and dad sat on either side of me trying to comfort me. I was numb, and they took it as me being in shock. They were half right. The apathy that Sophia, my love, had almost rid me of had returned. I didn't know how to react. The world again seemed meaningless and dead to me.

After all of the families in attendance had paid their respects and gone out to the burial site, I stayed behind and asked my parents to leave. Sophia's parents were generous and allowed me to have some privacy with her. I approached her open casket and studied her beautiful features for the last time. It was the first time I had seen a dead human body. She looked relatively the same, but pale, and quiet. I wanted to touch her skin but knew that it was inappropriate. The longer I examined her, the more my chest began to ache. I realized that that one person, a person who accepted me for who I was, was never going to show up to work again, standing by my side; playfully bumping her hip into mine when the customers weren't looking. I would never hear her childhood stories or her silly jokes again. I lost control. Tears streamed down my face, falling onto her soft hands that were folded over one another. I whispered to her, asking her why she left me, even though I knew it was a silly question that couldn't be answered. As I stood there, rage that I know all too well now, the rage I had not felt since I was in the psychiatric hospital consumed me.

Sophia had been killed in a car accident by another senior at our high school. She was coming home from work the previous Saturday night in her compact car, the night that I called in sick after catching the flu. As she was passing through a stop light, the kid, Charles Schmidt, driving a suburban, ran through his red light and smashed directly into the driver side door of Sophia's car going sixty miles an hour. She was killed instantly from the impact. Charles made it out alive with just a few scrapes and bruises, as the airbag had protected him from the impact.

After the funeral, I couldn't stop thinking about Sophia, how much she had meant to me, how she had taught me what love was. I would lay awake in my bed, night after night, holding my pillow tightly, pretending it was her. Who knows what could have been? We could have gone off to the same school, gotten married, and even had a family.

Charles, the foolish murderer, became the focus of my pain, of my rage. The thought of hurting him got me out of bed each day. I knew I would have to be smart about it, as I would not want to be caught and put in jail. I planned carefully for weeks, following him home, studying him from afar, and eavesdropping on people talking about him. Everyone had said that he had become withdrawn and depressed, that he was remorseful and had begged her family for forgiveness. Those things were not enough. I could not forgive him, and I would never forget. However, all of my plans had been interrupted by Charles himself.

Just days before I was going to sneak into his house and suffocate him in his sleep, he approached me. It was around eight-thirty on a Wednesday night and I was sitting at the top of the school bleachers in front of the football field by myself, thinking about Sophia. I was lost in space and then a weak, timid voice called my name.

"John... John Sullivan, is that you up there?"

I lifted my head from my knees and as I did Charles Schmidt's eyes met mine. I wasn't sure how to respond as that had not been part of the plan and was totally unexpected.

Without knowing what to do I just nodded, and after I did he made his way up to the top of the bleachers where I sat and stood next to me. He started crying before he even spoke, his lips quivering with each word.

"John... I'm so sorry for what I've done... I had to get my dad's truck home and I just barely missed the light. I didn't see anyone coming so... I just sped through... and it... just happened... Please... forgive me... I'm so sorry..."

He sobbed loudly as he spoke and his head lowered in shame. After the shock of his unexpected visit wore off, the hatred began pulsing in my veins. I wasn't sure what I was going to do exactly, but I knew I was going to kill him. As I gathered my wits and explored my options, he continued talking, gaining some control over his emotions, but still weeping as he spoke. His curly red hair bounced around as his scrawny frame shuttered from the sobs.

"I came out here to think about what I've done, to talk to God… to try to figure this whole thing out… I think God sent me here today to make peace with you, you know? I don't think this is a chance encounter… I need you to forgive me… So that Sophia…"

When the name of my love fell from his lips I stood up quickly and faced him, interrupting him with my gaze. He just stood there sobbing, hoping that I would forgive him. I looked around in every direction checking for witnesses. I saw no one. Adrenaline took control and I grabbed him by the neck with both hands and squeezed with every ounce of strength that I had. His eyes looked into my own, his terror, his weakness only fueled the hatred. He struggled and tried to pull my hands away, but it only made me squeeze harder. After a few seconds he fell to his knees, his eyes pleading for me to let go. I leaned down and growled in his face "Fuck your God!"

After two or three minutes, I let go of his neck. His limp body slumped before me and as the adrenaline died down I realized I had a serious problem. If I didn't want to go jail, *I had to find a way to make this work*, as I would surely be questioned by the police before anyone, if not first, it would be immediately after Sophia's father.

Looking around I could see that my options were limited. Then I saw it. A large plastic banner twenty feet down from me was hanging over the guard rail of the bleachers. There was about ten feet of thick white rope holding it in place. I could create a noose from it and make it appear to be a suicide. That is exactly what I did. After pulling the rope out of the grommet holes I wadded up the banner and tossed it to the side. I then quickly looped up a noose from the rope, a thing that I had practiced many times before for one of my animal experiments.

I put the loop around his neck and secured the other end to the guard rail. With one final look to make sure no one saw, I picked Charles up and dumped him over the edge. His neck snapped as his body came to a halt. He was dead for sure, and I had cleaned up my mistake. Everyone would think that he was overcome with guilt and couldn't handle it anymore.

I walked through the darkness of night back to my father's car and was fortunate enough to leave the parking lot unnoticed. Charles, his limp corpse slowly moving back and forth, would also go unnoticed until the following morning. I remember being woken up by my mother, her voice shaky and gentle as she spoke to me.

"John... Wake up honey... Don't worry about getting out of bed; school has been canceled for the day..."

Her voice trailed off as I set up and asked her why. She didn't want to answer me but I continued to prod her. Even though I knew the reason, I did not want to appear suspicious. After a few moments of silence she finally responded. "Charles Schmidt, a boy from your school, the same boy who had the accident with Sophia... He committed suicide last night on the school grounds... He hung himself from the bleachers by the football field... The police do not want any students on the campus until everything has been taken care of... You go on back to sleep and have some rest. We'll talk about it later, OK sweetie?"

I nodded at my gentle mother and played dumb; laying my head back onto the pillow I had been pretending was Sophia for so many days and nights. My mother sat next to me silently, stroking my hair, trying to comfort me though I felt nothing. If only she knew the truth. I shut my eyes and went back to sleep.

Over the next few months my mind kept going back to the kill. I would lock my bedroom door and turn up my stereo all the way as I strangled my bedpost, reliving the emotions I felt as Charles Schmidt slowly died by my hands. The surge of anger and hatred was very powerful. It felt like there was electricity running through every avenue of my bloodstream, and had I not been so intent on receiving immediate gratification, I would have been able to enjoy the process properly. The visualization, the new and wonderful emotions, the loud music, it all came together; it became an art form that I have still yet to perfect...

Ah, memories. I did miss the proper love of a woman; I missed it terribly, though I would not openly admit it to anyone. I didn't just miss it, I needed it. I'd been slowly killing myself, trying to mask the ailment that was my first love. I would find another... I just needed to rest.

Chapter 8: Aggression

After opening my eyes I realized that I was laying belly down on my bedroom carpet. I got up and as I did it became clear that I had pissed myself during my long nap. The smell was strong, and as my legs fully extended I could feel my pubic hair pulling away from my genitals. I must have been out for a long time for the urine to have become crusted. I checked the alarm clock on the other side of my bed and saw that it was eleven-thirty p.m. I was almost out for twenty four hours that time... *Fuck, I was supposed to work today.* I'd leave my boss a voice mail with some bullshit story about family problems. He'd buy it; he seemed to like me alright. Fuck it, I'd take the rest of the week off, I had work to do.

A nice long shower helped me clear my head. Upon entering the bathroom I flipped the light switch up and turned on the water. After disrobing I wasted no time and hopped right into the cold, sobering streams of liquid. The shock of the temperature gave me a jolt and woke me up completely.

I dried off and finished the hygienic routine I had perfected over the years, but decided to put deodorant on right then, not after I had a shirt on. It was time for me to start making some changes. That part of the routine was now officially changed forever, it was gone. I'd put deodorant on before my clothing from that day forth and that was the end of it.

Opening my dresser drawer I scanned through the minimal selection of old clothes and did not see anything I felt like wearing. *Fuck it.* I didn't need any clothes right then; no plans could have been put into motion until daylight. I began pacing back and forth, and as I did an unusual burst of energy surged through my entire being. I felt incredible... so strong. I wanted to lift something heavy; I wanted to move my body around with rigorous effort.

After unlocking the door, I ran down the steps into the basement where an old weight set sitting off in the corner had been collecting dust for the last two years. I turned the radio up loud. Hard rock screamed out to me, commanding me to act with aggression. I put one hundred and fifty pounds on the bench press and slid underneath. As the weight was pushed up, and then lowered to my chest I anticipated great resistance, but there was none, no shoulder pain, no shaky arms, nothing, just raw power. I pressed it up multiple times with ease but it was simply not adequate for my current needs. After adding another fifty pounds I repeated the process. It was challenging but still not enough to break a sweat. I was literally throwing the weight up, set after set after set. Still there was no sense of satisfaction.

The jump rope hanging on the wall caught my eye. That would help cool me out and burn some of the energy. Right away I swung it up and then under as fast as I could. Ten, fifteen, thirty minutes went by. Still, I was raging, I was alive. I threw the rope to the ground and grabbed the pull-up bar. My bodyweight offered little resistance as I pulled myself upward. A vicious, guttural battle cry was forced out by my working lungs with each repetition. I was not counting I was just going, and going.

I lost interest in the pull-ups and ran up the basement stairs that lead out into the backyard. There was a six foot log lying next to the shed that the landlord had left behind while clearing some trees beyond the fence line. I estimated that it weighed about two hundred and fifty pounds, maybe more. My body demanded that I pick it up, and then drop it, over and over. I did not deny the pleasure that my flesh commanded.

A half hour or so had passed and I laid naked in the grass staring up at what few stars I could see through the filthy

New Jersey sky. I imagined what it would look like if there wasn't smog and light pollution blocking my view. I had a fairly good idea as I had seen the heavens in all their glory at Yosemite National Park. That was the image I chose to see. I imagined how my Norse ancestors felt as they laid in the battlefield waiting for dawn to break so that they could kill again. It fascinated me. The possibility of defeat, yet the confidence of certain victory... That was the attitude to have. *Victory is certain, and if it isn't, fuck it, let Odin decide what to do with me next.*

Though I did not believe that Odin was in fact a real entity, I liked the idea behind his teachings. Never accept defeat, fear nothing, remorse not for your slain enemy, and kill everything keeping you from your objective. At least that is what I remembered reading about Odin. If I was wrong about my history, so be it, I was in control, I was in the driver's seat, I would make ideology conform to me.

The deeper my thoughts went the less anxious I felt. I needed to slow down a bit and develop the new mentality that had been bestowed upon me. I needed to change my persona, the attitude that the outside world would see... that women would see. I had always admired the coolness of James Dean and considered his level of likeability timeless. *Yes, that was it* I thought to myself. My new image would be modeled after Mr. Dean. I would shave and get a haircut in the morning to start the process. After that I would go to the nearest shopping mall and pick up the correct clothing. The final step would be to gather a collection of all Dean's Hollywood work and study it carefully. That would take some time but ultimately it would be necessary.

It wouldn't do me any good to steal his lines, as people would easily pick up on it, it just wouldn't seem right considering it had been nearly sixty years since his death. No,

I would just need to move like him, use his facial expressions, his way with women, his way with people, all of it. There was a certain way to walk, to pause in conversation, to give a glance here and a shrug there; those would be the type of things I would need to develop. However, I could not just simply spend a week or two studying and then instantly implement the style; it would be a slow progression so that it would go mostly unnoticed. I had been too introverted, too confusing to others to simply change overnight. Yes, that was a sound and well thought out plan.

My planning was interrupted by a large dog that was sniffing at something near my feet. As my head rose to meet the gaze of the curious animal it snarled and snapped at what it then perceived to be a threat. Normally I would have been startled by such a sight. No matter. I quickly worked out the mathematics of the situation. I was more than twice its weight and knew that I could defend myself from the likely assault. The new found threat potentially had rabies so I had to be agile and avoid any fluid contact.

As I jumped to my feet the creature rushed forward. Its jaws snapped at my leg but I was too swift. I retaliated with a vicious stomp of my foot, crushing its heads with the heel. It lied before me, spasms contorted its body and blood ran from its mouth. I examined my handy work but was not totally satisfied with the outcome. The log, yes that was perfect; I would crush its body as a display of dominance.

I was then fully feeling the tiring effects of my workout but knew that I could lift the massive hunk of wood one more time. With a deep and powerful grunt I hoisted the log onto my shoulder and then slammed the end of it down onto my battle opponent with every ounce of strength that I had. Innards shot from its rectum and its head had become unusually flat. It was done. I had won the fight and come out unscathed. The victory did not bring much satisfaction, and certainly no glory, but it also brought no discontent. I snatched the curious little bastard by the back of his broken neck and tossed him off into the woods for the wilderness to dispose of.

Eight hours had passed and I spent them on the internet reading about Socrates and various other great thinkers. I would work their ideas into my new systematic approach of living life and bonding with a woman. Great wisdom could win a man many battles in the world, and I'd need to continually expand my horizons if I was going to fulfill my ambitions as a modern day Viking, a Viking that valued knowledge as much as raw power.

As I entered the shopping mall the aroma of the food court was enticing, but I would eat later, I had a lot of work to do and so little time. Various breeds of people passed by, ranging from hip-hop ethnic types to snooty looking white Suburbanites. Skater kids with greasy hair, big shoes, and torn pants ran about causing harmless mayhem as all little shits do, bumping into old people, throwing candy at each other, stealing. Ah, but there was something much more interesting, and that was all of the lovely women walking around in clothing that some rich fool, whether it be a Daddy, or a sucker of a husband had paid for. Perhaps I jumped to conclusions too quickly; some of them surely were highly educated professionals. That was jealousy I was feeling, I needed to calm down and focus on my objective.

One extraordinarily beautiful woman standing behind the counter of a small coffee shop caught my eye and I decided it would be best to take a seat on a nearby bench so that I may study her further. She looked to be about twenty-five and her hair was a healthy, silky blonde, feathered and flowing down near the top of her breast. I couldn't tell the color of her eyes, at least not for certain, but they were either green or blue for sure. Overall her facial bone structure was perfect. It was very feminine. She was talking to a new customer in the store and laughing about something. As her mouth opened and closed I could see that she had a small gap between her two front teeth, which were perfectly white. That aroused me a great deal. A woman who was beautiful but had a slight flaw was wonderfully attractive, just simply delectable.

Let me not get hung up on one detail though, there was more to see as she walked from behind the counter and out into the open. That allowed for a full examination of her body. She was slender and wearing a correctly fitted summer dress with a flower pattern on it. Her breasts were small but well-proportioned to her frame. As she swirled I could see her buttocks and the back of her legs. Her ass was magnificent as I had assumed it was. But, there was one thing left, the ankles. Some women have thicker ankles and that was a thing that I did not particularly find attractive, though I would likely not have let it be the deciding factor in courtship.

This creature did not adorn those ankles though. They were of normal size and again made my heart race with passion. Her skin, how could I forget? It was pale, the healthy kind... perhaps milky would be better to describe it. Yes, her skin was milky and smooth; free of blemishes as far as I could tell, and I had no doubt that it was soft and smooth to the touch.

I hadn't approached a woman sober in many years, mostly out of fear I suppose. I felt none at that moment. With the fresh shave, the haircut I had gotten before I came, and the basic black t-shirt, blue jeans, and white shoes, I looked fairly normal. I thought to myself *I'll go over and say hello*. If she was accepting of my mannerisms... Ah yes, mannerisms... That woman did not know me, so going full throttle James Dean did not put me in danger of discovery as it would from my peers at work. I had to take it easy though, I hadn't watched a Dean flick in a long time. Cool and confident, powerful eyes… that would be sufficient.

As I approached the counter that she was once again standing behind she greeted me with her adorable smile. I smiled back and said "hi". Women are much savvier than many men give them credit for, at least some of them are, and I sensed that she knew I wanted to flirt with her. I saw no signs of worry or disgust, just big, innocent, green eyes looking into mine. I didn't want to get crazy though. A little small talk, a coffee that I wouldn't drink, and a goodbye would suffice.

Her response to my greeting was as expected. Her voice was so tender… so sweet.

"Hi, what can I get for you?"

I scanned over the menu behind her, a chalk board filled with big, loopy, girly handwriting. I really didn't know anything about coffee…

"Can I just get a small black coffee with sugar and cream?" My tone was that of a man who had just received a blow-job, mellow, and in no rush to do anything. The words passed my lips with ease and I could see that she enjoyed the sound of my voice. She looked into my eyes and then down at my lips before replying.

"Sure thing sweetie, would you like any napkins?" I hadn't thought about that. I couldn't think of any reason that I would need napkins as I was going to throw the coffee away as soon as I was out of her sight. *I'd better take them though* I thought to myself, maybe something would come up later and I'd need them.

"Yeah, I'll take some napkins."

I nodded my head slowly and gave her about fifty percent of the Dean facial expression that most appropriately fit the situation.

I paid her and she handed me the coffee with the napkins. The cup was extremely hot and my nervous system was insisting that I put it down at once and wrap the napkins around the exterior of the cup; however, I was already fully committed to holding it. If I yelped and put it down, it could make her feel insecure about her abilities to serve coffee properly, I did not want that. Her first emotional experience with me needed to be one hundred percent positive. If I was ever going to mate with the goddess before me I needed to carefully calculate each move.

I told her "Thank you." And she replied kindly "You're welcome, I hope you enjoy it! Have a good day!" I nodded my head, made a slow turn while still maintaining eye contact and then just walked away; perfection...

Chapter 9: Transmute

It had been three months since I had decided to find love again. No whisky, wholesome foods, and a sound exercise regimen had transformed my body back into the rock-hard form it once was. Prior to my self-loathing, two year-long whisky binge, I had exercised rigorously to better fit in with a healthy crowd. This time I did it with a true purpose. I wanted my future companion, Linda, to love me. My James Dean persona still needed some work, but by reducing my physical flaws to a bare minimum, there would be more for her to work with.

I had spoken to her seventeen times since our first meeting and had confirmed that she was not married, or currently dating anyone. It had been very challenging to have conversations with her, but she had been most helpful in the process. She started noticing that I was losing weight about two months into the transformation and commented on it. I still remember her sweet words.

"Wow, John! Every time I see you, you look better than the last! I wish I had your discipline to eat right… but I just can't seem to give up the truffles we sell here."

She looked beautiful as she said it… I enjoyed the sound of the word *truffle* after she said it, and from that day forth I would associate that word with positive emotions.

Though our conversations had indeed been brief, I had made some progress toward the goal of companionship. She knew that my income was bordering upper middle class, that I was a military veteran, and that I had attended some college classes. I was modest in disclosing that information as I did not want to sound like a braggart, or for lack of a better term, like a complete douche bag. I wanted her to know that I was successful by the standards American society had come up with, and that I would be able to provide a reasonable living for us if we were to take things to the highest level.

In return, I learned that she was attending nursing school while working at the coffee shop. Her father was deceased and she currently resided at her mother's home just twenty minutes from my own. She also told me that she had no siblings, her favorite food was Mexican, and that she often watched scary movies while she was alone on the weekends. I had considered those facts carefully and was still figuring out how to take advantage of that knowledge. I did not want to ask her on a date to eat Mexican food and then take her to a scary movie, as that would just be too forward, like I was bowing to her desires. I needed to make it equal on both sides of the house if it was going to work. I needed to present a challenge. I needed her to chase me.

Unfortunately I was at a disadvantage, as my hobbies, if that is what they would be named as, were mutilating the bodies of societies dregs, exercising until I reached complete exhaustion, and studying James Dean. I told her that when I was not fixing aircraft, I enjoyed working on cars, traveling on the weekends, and that my favorite genre of movies was drama. I was certain that I could have done a little better than that, but I covered the basics required to appear manly, adventurous, and thoughtful. That is what I wanted her to see.

I had to study maps, locations, automotive repair, and watch dozens of dramas to ensure that Linda did not catch me in a lie. That had taken a great deal of time, as I had no interest or background in any of those subjects. And on top of that, my continued transformation into Mr. Dean still required practice each day. After my workouts, when I was most relaxed, I stood in front of the mirror and worked on my reactions, facial expressions, and terminology. I also had to perfect my walk which required a video camera, and then more time critiquing the footage.

Those extra activities, as necessary as they were, had gotten in the way of my other passion. I still had not fully planned out how I was going to rid the world of Jebediah Winston Tarner, the snake toothed hillbilly from the grocery store. He had sexually assaulted at least one woman and one child. I suspected he had harmed more and the incidents were never reported. Predators do not tend to stop, they grow into true monsters if they are not detained or destroyed. I had to get rid of him soon, for I feared he may strike again if he hadn't already.

I was going to study an automotive manual on that night, but I had to stay focused on the more important task. My knowledge as of then was passable but would still require some polish. If a situation unfolded with Linda where I had no real answers about automobile maintenance I would just have to dance around the topic before slyly changing it. I had three hours until my new scheduled bed time of three a.m. The remainder of the night would be fully dedicated to the project I had put off for too long. Jebediah Winston Tarner now had my full attention.

Chapter 10: Consecrate

It had been a long day at work. I missed my scheduled morning exercise session. My boss called me early in the morning, waking me from my slumber. He apologized and asked if I'd like to get some overtime. I was hesitant but he persisted, nearly to the point of begging. I caved into his request as he had always treated me fairly.

Fast forward sixteen hours later and I was exhausted, but I refused to sleep before my exercise routine had been completed. I stopped to get an energy drink before going home. That would give me enough juice to conquer the heavy weights that silently awaited my return.

As I entered the convenient store I waved to the Korean cashier who I had started calling by first name, Yong, which was short for Yong-sun. I was curious of its origins so I did some research and found that it meant dragon in first position. It was fitting of his character, as he was a pleasant and hardworking man. I had no doubt that he did everything in his power to provide the best life for his family.

As I pulled the can from the cooler I heard a loud and obnoxious ghetto accent coming from behind me. I headed back up toward the cashier, examining the creature that had disturbed the peace as he entered the store. He was a short and sloppy looking black man in his late twenties. His attire consisted of baggy jeans, a hooded sweat jacket, and cheap jewelry dangling from his neck. He was yelling into a pre-paid cellphone... Rubbish about someone who better have his money, being theatrical with his free hand as he spoke.

I approached the counter and reached for my wallet, but was stopped short by the imbecile as he stepped in front of me and started barking at my friend, Yong, requesting the location of toothpaste. Yong politely pointed to the aisle that had the requested item. The ghetto trash walked away in the direction of Yong's finger, bumping into my shoulder as he did. A flash of rage, which was not as easy to control with my raised testosterone levels from the clean diet and exercise regimen, warmed my skin. I did not make eye contact though, or say excuse me. Instead, I thought of Linda, she was my main focus, and any interaction with that idiot could cause unnecessary problems that would interfere with my free time.

"Hey, John, how are you? It isn't too often I see you in here this late, must have been a long day at work, huh?"

I smiled at Yong and nodded my head *yes*, chuckling and gesturing as James Dean would. He replied sympathetically, sighing as he did "Yeah, I know that feeling…"

Just as I finished paying, our friendly formalities were interrupted by heavy breathing that reeked of alcohol, which was coming from directly over my shoulder. It was the fucking dreg.

"Yo, my man, Bruce Lee, I don't see no motha fuckin toothpaste back there! Why don't you come show me where it's at? Come on nigga, I aint got all god damn night, move yo little Chinese legs!"

Yong pointed again and explained that it was right next to the medication, on the right side of the aisle. The man was not pleased by his response, staring at him with the intent of intimidation. Yong just smiled in reply, trying to calm the man.

"You think this is funny China man, huh? How about you white boy? Say something motha fucka! I wish you would… come on, nigga, test me!"

I could think of nothing relevant to say, nor did I care to continue smelling his awful, drunken stench. Turning my head back, I replied evenly. "No, I have nothing to say." As I finished my sentence he became excitable and reached into his filthy sweat jacket, pulling out a small black gun. It occurred to me that he had set us up, that he needed both of us to be in front of him so that he could maintain control. I should have been more observant, my obsession over Linda had become too distracting. I was getting sloppy.

He nervously pointed the gun at Yong, yelling loudly as he did "Open the register motha fucka!" He then pointed the gun at me and demanded that I get face down on the floor. I did as he said and began evaluating the situation.

He was intoxicated, showed no signs of athleticism, and was obviously of much lesser intelligence; however, he did have what appeared to be a loaded gun and was probably stupid enough to use it. I laid quietly, watching his every move in the reflection of the glass double doors. Yong quickly opened the drawer and began stacking the bills on the counter. As he did the thug was displeased with the amount and made another demand. "The safe, motha fucka! Open the god-damn-safe!" Yong replied coolly and respectfully. "It is in the supply room, we'll have to go there to get it." I was impressed with Yong's ability to handle the situation, as I knew he had been robbed at least three times since I'd been coming to the store.

The two-bit piece of shit robber yanked the back of my shirt and pulled me up from the floor so that I was standing in front of him. "Come on, white boy!" I did as instructed, remaining calm and quiet. When we got into the supply room I was pushed to the floor and told to sit down and shut the fuck up. The gun was pointed about three inches from Yong's head as he kneeled down by a stack of large boxes and slid them to the side, making the safe visible. He turned the knob a few times back and forth and the door popped open. Neither myself, nor our ghetto hostage-taker could see its contents.

Yong shuffled his hands around inside of the large metal box, and then, to my surprise turned around with a pistol and shot the robber in the shin. It was clear by Yong's lack of accuracy, and his eyes looking away as he shot, that he did not want to hurt other people and that he was terrified. The robber to my left, screamed as the bullet lodged itself deep behind his shin bone. He returned fire and shot Yong in the upper back before I got ahold of his weapon and began struggling for control.

The sudden expression of panic, the weakness of the thug... It drove me wild, I was possessed, I was the wolf, and he was the little rabbit. As our arms tangled together I forced the gun off to one side, pointing it at the wall. He looked at me with fear in his eyes, desperately, and then at the gun. Without hesitation I took the opening and bit his nose, ripping at it with my front teeth. The tip gave way and I spit it to the floor. The sudden shock to his nervous system and realization that I had disfigured him gave me the advantage. We tumbled to the floor and I landed on top, yanking the gun from his hands and stuffing it into his mouth.

Yong had flipped over and was watching both of us, his face scrunched up tightly from the pain. The robber's saliva coated my trigger finger as I buried the muzzle deeper into his throat. He could see it in my eyes; he knew he was not leaving the room alive. I had not killed in months. I used that opportunity to feed my desires. I would watch him tremble.

The room was quiet, all except for the sounds of terrified, drunken breathing.

I pulled the trigger. Yong screamed as the blast pierced our ears. The back of the robber's cranium emptied its contents onto the linoleum floor beneath me. With intense satisfaction I examined him, studying his contorted face carefully. My moment was interrupted by the sensation of wetness around my lower abdomen. *Shit, I was bleeding.*

"John Sullivan! Over here! Can you walk us through what transpired here and how you responded to the situation?"

Cameras flashed over and over as three microphones were held in front of my face by reporters. The paramedics, just minutes earlier, had removed the bullet fragment from my lower abdomen. I sat shirtless with a bandage covering the small wound. Initially it looked worse than it actually was. It had only sliced my skin, not even enough for stiches. They insisted that I go to the hospital for a full checkup and blood tests, but I declined. I just wanted to go home and start my exercise routine.

I stared at the reporters in silence, hoping they would get the hint that I was in a rush. They didn't seem to care. I realized that my boss, my parents, and most importantly, Linda, would see me on the news as it was likely going to be a popular story. I chose my words carefully, utilizing the coolness of James Dean as I spoke.

"It was an unfortunate… engagement… Mr. Yong-sun and I were put into a situation that neither of asked to be in… If Yong had not had the courage to use the gun from his safe, we could have both been murdered… I am grateful to him and wish him a quick recovery."

The reporters were not content with my answer and shouted over one another with more questions, wanting to know the details of how I had killed the robber. The truth was that I relished in it. I hated him from the moment I saw him.

I answered as vaguely as I could. "I saw an opportunity that would allow Mr. Yong-sun and I to live, and I took it." As the last word passed my lips I stood up and exited the rear door of the ambulance and walked away from the reporters, ignoring their questions as I did. As I approached the police officers walking around the yellow tape in front of the store, the reporters were pushed back. The detective running the show had me sign my statement and confirm my contact information. He encouraged me once again to go to the hospital for a blood test, as the robber may have had HIV. I told him that I would go first thing in the morning... that I just needed to get home and rest. I thanked him for his concern and walked back to my vehicle, making no eye contact with the reporters as I did.

As the barbell rose from my chest I exhaled and pushed hard. The excitement that had taken place earlier had worn off and was hardly worth thinking about. I had a new problem on my hands. It occurred to me that Linda might be intimidated by the fact that I had killed a man. It was true that it was in self-defense, and that all of it was captured by the surveillance cameras in the convenient store. I would be labeled as a hero in the public eye. However, it did not change the fact that I took a life. It could truly go either way. She may want to treat me with sympathy and admiration, or she may become withdrawn and afraid of me, not wanting to discuss it at all. *Fuck... everything could be ruined between us...* No, I'd come too far, I'd built myself back up into something that mattered. I would need to do some research.

The first thing I would look into was how soldiers reintegrated into society after coming home from war. I knew that the personnel who had to kill in combat zones received briefings and professional counseling to help them readjust to a peaceful environment. It was highly likely that those counseling sessions provided specific, well-thought-out advice on how to talk with their loved ones about the tragedies that took place. Yes, that would be the best possible avenue. That was what I would do. I would study every article and every video I could find online regarding the subject before seeing Linda again.

Chapter 11: Love

It had been nine days since I'd dispatched of the robber. As I drove toward the mall I went over the answers to the possible questions Linda would ask me. I suspected that she would respond well, but it was difficult to predict, as the thought process of a woman is something science has yet to figure out. If the worst case scenario took place, in which Linda hinted that she was afraid of me... I would dig up that ghetto-scum piece of shit and force his family to eat him.

Linda saw me walking toward the coffee shop from a distance and placed a sign on the counter that read "I'll be back in fifteen minutes!" She adjusted the small cardboard clock attached to the sign and then rushed toward me. Her eyes were those of concern, and to my surprise she hugged me tightly as we met. The warmth of her touch and her enticing perfume threw me off guard. It was the first time we had made physical contact, a thing I did not suspect would take place until I had successfully asked her out on a date.

Gently I placed my arms around her, but did not want to go too far, and decided to let her take the lead. Without letting go of my torso she pulled her head from my chest and gazed into my eyes as she spoke, her tone as sweet as could be.

"I saw you on the news... are you alright? When you were talking to the reporters there was a bandage on your stomach... were you... shot?" Her eyes moistened as she awaited my response.

I felt fortunate she had made the scenario so simple. I replied appreciatively "I'm doing good... a small fragment from the bullet ricochet gave me a little cut, but it is nothing really. It is almost fully healed now." I lifted my shirt just enough to show her the wound that looked more like a scrape after nine days of healing. She sighed in relief and then asked me if I wanted to take a walk with her. I smiled and told her "I'd love to."

Linda led me through two large metal doors that opened up into a hallway where the mall employees could pass through to their break area outside. After exiting the building we walked over to a large wooden bench that was placed under a canopy. We were alone at last. There were no prying eyes from the world, no distractions from busy shoppers; it was just Linda and I.

She sat on the bench first, grabbing my fingers gently, much like a child wood, and gestured for me to sit next to her. I was a little flustered as I was not sure where the conversation would go. I had expected that encounter, at best, to be similar to our previous, where we would stand at the counter of her shop for no more than ten minutes and talk politely, both being coy with our flirtation. Before I could begin searching through my memory for answers I had rehearsed she began speaking to me.

"I was so worried when I saw the news. I felt sick to my stomach… seeing the bandage on you, and the reporters… my God, the questions they were asking you after everything that had happened. I can't even imagine how horrifying it all was… And you looked so strong and handsome, and the way you answered them, it was like a movie…"

Still holding her hand I took the opportunity to utilize Mr. Dean's coolness. I knew that if I responded appropriately I could remove the murderous distraction from our developing relationship.

"It was pretty scary, but I am slowly moving past it… I feel like the luckiest man on earth. Every day since then, when I wake up, I want to make each moment count… I don't ever want to put anything off again no matter what it is…"

Linda interrupted me, and without warning placed her warm lips against my own as she thoughtfully caressed my chest. She tasted wonderful. I hadn't had that feeling, the current of love surging through my veins, in far too long. The hard work, the studying…rehearsing, returning my body to a healthy state… it had all paid off. A woman who would have likely not given me a second look just a few short months ago had fallen for me. I had reached my first goal.

After the passionate moment expired she pulled away slowly and began to cry, burying her face in her hands. Affectionately I rubbed her middle back and waited for her to decide which direction to go from there. I didn't want to tell her it was all going to be alright, as I couldn't be certain why she was crying. I suspected it was not only from the excitement of seeing me again after I could have been killed, but from the embarrassment of our first kiss; her lack of control in my presence. Under the circumstances that seemed logical. However, the tears could have been those of regret.

She sobbed as the jumbled words left her perfect lips "I'm so sorry… You have been through so much and I couldn't sleep… I've been thinking about you every night … I didn't mean to do that… I just wanted to be close to you…"

Now is my chance I thought to myself. I knew what the man I had modeled my new persona after would do. With all confidence and no hesitation I placed my hand on the back of her neck and pulled her gently toward me, pausing just before our lips met, letting her see the care and sincerity in my eyes. And then we kissed, that time more passionately. She responded well to my dominant move and pressed her tongue into my mouth. It was silky and tasted like bubblegum. If there was a heaven, that would have been it for me. That was exactly the way I felt with Sophia, the exact feeling I had been longing for.

Many minutes passed as we held each other, neither one of us wanting to be the first to pull away. I never wanted the moment to end, but it would soon. It was necessary for me to continue being both patient, and strict in my new found discipline for our love to progress. The foundation for success had been laid and to fuck it up then would have been more than foolish.

After our moment of passion expired she slowly sat back and took a deep breath, exhaling with a cute feminine noise following it. Her eyes were glassy as she peered into my own. The moment was interrupted by a dirty word coming from a lovely mouth.

"Shit, I'm sorry; I have to get back to the coffee shop... John, when will I see you again?" I smiled and replied coolly "How about Saturday... would you like to go to dinner? I know a place I think you would enjoy." Without thought she replied with an excited "Yes!" Taking my hand, she jotted down her number and address on my palm and told me to call her with the plans. With that, she kissed me on the cheek, got up, and headed back toward the metal double doors. Looking back, she gave me a final wink and then disappeared into the building.

I was grateful that she had left me alone and did not ask for me to walk her back to work. I had a raging hard-on that I couldn't force down. If I would have stood up and walked into the building with Linda, there was no doubt she would have seen it. We were nowhere near that comfort stage yet. I just sat there for a while and let it die down before heading back inside.

Since everything with Linda had been settled I could free my mind up and focus on the task that had been put off for far too long. I needed to get back to work on Jebediah. I had most of the tools I would need to properly exercise that demon; however, there was still a missing component. I wanted to try a new method during the operation and I would need to head to the hardware store to acquire the correct tooling.

The hardware store was a place that I had become fond of. It was my armory. Nearly every weapon and tool I needed to combat the scum of the world could be found there. Saws, hammers, knives, chains, chemicals… it was perfect.

As I walked through the lumber section I read the labels until I found what I was searching for; hardwood dowel closet-poles. I took one from the tall standing rack and inspected it for defects. After a close examination none could be found. It was perfect.

While standing at the cash register I heard someone calling me by my last name. It was a man's voice, familiar in tone. I turned to see who it was and from behind a sea of people a short, tubby man emerged.

"Hey, Sullivan, is that you? Holy shit man I hardly recognized you… you look like a fucking super hero, what the hell happened? I haven't seen you in like six months." Had I cared about his observation I would have been flattered. The man was Carl Smith, another civilian who worked on the night shift back at the aircraft hangar. His shop was right next to mine. I had also seen him at the mutant bar on occasion. We had exchanged military stories along with generic, bullshit drunk-talk.

I responded politely "Hey Carl, long time no-see. Yeah, I had to let go of the alcohol man, it was taking up too much money and the doc said my liver could use a rest." He snickered at my lie.

"Shit man, good job! A few guys were telling me you haven't been hanging out much anymore and that you were all hard core with the gym shit. Well, that's cool man, I'm happy for you. I gotta get back to work, the old lady made me get a second job once she found out she was pregnant... Anyway, it was good seeing you Sully, take it easy brother."

I replied "likewise" and nodded my head. I was glad he was working there and not a customer in line behind me. Listening to his nonsense about fixing up the piece of shit hot rod in his garage was painful to say the least, and regardless of the conversation level he always found a way to sneak it in.

After paying the cashier and loading the long wooden pole into my car, scratching the interior as I did, I headed back home to craft it into the tool I would be using on Jebediah. As I drove along the freeway I thought about how everything had changed. My adopted persona no longer felt forced, or fake. I had truly transformed into something new, I had matured not only in my actions, but in my thought process. There was still an impulse that I had to keep under control, but it didn't seem to trigger quite as often. It had to be Linda's doing.

I was able to stay focused on the tasks that did not concern her, but I wondered how long that would last. If we made love what would happen to me? What if it went well and we eventually decided to move in together, or even get married? How or where was I going to dispose of the mutants, the dregs that plagued society? If she ever found out, or even suspected it, I had no doubt she would leave me, and even go to the police.

I was getting ahead of myself. I hadn't even gotten through our first date yet. She wouldn't find out, she would never know. I would keep my eyes open for new places... new ways... *Fuck*.

The asshole in front of me slammed on his brakes, and though I saw it coming, I was unable to slow down. I smashed into the back of his prissy sport utility vehicle. The airbag exploded from the steering wheel and smashed my body against the seat. The windshield shattered. I think I blacked out for a split second. I was having trouble breathing, but I did not hear or feel any ribs crack upon impact. No, I just had the wind taken from me. I would be fine.

After forcing air back into my lungs I got out of the car and met the driver who slammed on his brakes in front of me. He jumped out of his vehicle, his face stricken with fear and panic. He looked like a college student with his University t-shirt, cargo shorts, backwards hat, and sandals.

"Dude, I'm so sorry! I dropped my cell-phone and… and when I went to pick it up I had to move my foot and I hit the brake pedal on accident… I'm so fucking sorry, man, are you ok?"

I looked at him, and then at my middle class luxury vehicle. The front-end was totaled and the windshield was smashed. "Yeah, I'm aright. Are you? Was anyone else in the vehicle with you?"

"Yeah, I'm fine; I had my seat belt on… No, there is no one else with me, I was just going to pick up my girlfriend before this happened… Hey, just sit down and relax ok, buddy? I'll call the police, do you want an ambulance?"

"No, I think I just had the wind knocked out of me, I should be alright."

As the kid paced back and forth in front of me, apologizing between random "fucks" and "shits" two police vehicles arrived with a tow truck pulling up right behind them. The cops were excitable. The area, just thirty minutes from my home, wasn't known for its crime or traffic accidents.

"Mr. Sullivan?" The police officer was a large man with a perfect mustache and buzz cut. Before he saw my face he looked like a robot as so many police do, but I suppose I had become a bit of a celebrity recently. I replied "Yes, sir, that is my name." Wanting to get through the accident report and insurance exchange as quickly as possible, I answered respectfully and decisively.

"Wow, you've been through a lot recently, eh? Me and my partner were just talking about... what happened at the convenient..." His voice trailed off as he realized I may not have wanted to talk about it. I could see that he was waiting to gauge my reaction before continuing. He was correct, I did not want to talk about it as it was insignificant and would only prolong the process of me getting back to work on my project.

As I stared at him in silence he continued. "My apologies sir, are you injured?" I shook my head *no*. "That is good to hear... can I ask what happened here?" Before I could explain the situation the College kid, who identified himself as Cody, told the story. I was prepared for him to fabricate, or twist it so that it was in his favor, but he did just the opposite. The first words out of his mouth were that the accident was his fault. He explained dropping the cell phone, and called himself a "dumb fuck" multiple times as he went on. The police were trying to guide Cody away from me as he spoke so that they could get both sides of the story without us potentially shouting over one another, as many idiots do, but they ceased as the kid went on about it being his fault and how sorry he was. When he finished they asked him to wait in front of his vehicle so that they could speak with me in private.

"Mr. Sullivan, do you feel that his story is both accurate and true? Would you like to add anything?" I replied "What he says is true, but I think he may be being a bit hard on himself. He seems like a good kid. We've all been there, made silly mistakes..."

The police were content with our stories and filled out the accident reports. After the tow truck driver pulled my vehicle away the Police asked me if I needed a ride anywhere. I took them up on the offer as long as they did not mind me bringing the closet pole I had purchased. I told them a lie, that my girlfriend had been insisting that I fix the broken pole in her closet for some time, and I didn't want to come back with all bad news. They chuckled at my request and allowed me to bring it into the backseat of the cruiser.

As we headed back towards my house the cops began carefully dancing around the shooting, and the man I had killed not long ago. Their tone was that of pride, as if I had done them a service. I knew that by being vague, and offering them a small amount of entertainment, they would feel content and let it go. I also saw an opportunity to be friendly with the police, and that would likely come in handy in the future. It was clear at that point that my name was circulating in positive fashion amongst the officers in the surrounding precincts, and though I preferred to be unknown to the world, it was something that I could not control.

As I spoke I played into the character I knew they wanted me to be, the kind of asshole who was hamming it up for the camera of a shitty "true crime stories" television show. I was certain that neither one of those men had killed before, so they would not know the difference.

"I was afraid, but I knew that something had to be done or I wasn't going to walk out of that room... I can't really explain it... If I had to put it into words I would say that it was my military training, that sense of duty and honor. I swore to defend the constitution against enemies, both foreign and domestic, and that is what I did. That is what I had to do."

Even though I was a non-combatant during my service time... just an aircraft mechanic who only fired a gun in training twice, the military part would probably make those two cops, two guys who came across as armchair patriots, feel like they were in the presence of the kind of guy they heard about in country songs.

"Well, we sure do appreciate men like you. You make our job a hell of a lot easier… And we just want to thank you for your service, it really means a lot to us… Thank you… Mr. Sullivan… and I mean that." He tapped his heart with the palm of his hand as he said it.

Had I been capable, I would probably have blushed from how embarrassing the atmosphere had become, but I knew I had to play the game. I thanked them for their service as well, and entertained their nonsense until we reached my driveway.

The police officer driving the vehicle, *Buck*, saluted me as they pulled away. Finally I thought to myself. I didn't know how much more bullshit I could have listened to without losing my temper and ruining a good thing. Those guys were straight out of a bad movie. It was over, no sense in thinking about it further. I needed to get to work.

Chapter 12: Execution

As I stood there studying my newly acquired anatomy book on the work bench, or instrument table as I would like to refer to it as, Jebediah Winston Tarner, aka "Jeb", the redneck scum I encountered in the grocery store a few months back, laid on the table to my right. I'd secured his head in a vice attached to the table with just enough tension to keep it still.

His wide open eyes darted around the basement wildly and his limbs jerked violently against the leather straps holding them in place. I stuffed his filthy mouth with used socks and securely taped it shut. His muffled screams had been interrupting my concentration so I was forced to hit him in the throat with the rubber mallet that was amongst my many instruments of baptism. I had to be careful in my delivery, as I did not want to prematurely end his pathetic life. He just needed a warning. Though small whimpers could still be heard here and there, and the tension of twisting leather creaked at his resistance, it wasn't enough to distract me from my work. With a fine blend of early nineties grunge rock playing on the stereo I was able to fully tune him out.

Before the chloroform wore off I had cut away all of his clothing and cleaned his body thoroughly with bleach, as his smell was simply atrocious. His genitals were covered in warts and herpes sores, or at least that is what I assumed the open wounds were an indication of. I was fairly certain that he had more sexually transmitted diseases but was not qualified to say which. His fingernails were nearly chewed away but the toenails were longer than average, as I expected, and would be useful during the session. I'd selected a new tool that would work well for them.

I had been thinking about that moment for months, carefully planning each phase. From abducting him, to going unnoticed by my neighbors or any possible mutants that may be passing by deep into the night, it was all premeditated. When I found him he was already passed out in his shed, reeking of liquor and marijuana. I hand cuffed his arms and legs together behind his back and taped his mouth shut before dragging him to the trunk of my car. He awoke as I was getting him situated and tried to call out for help in his intoxicated haze. I was prepared for that and forced him to breath in chloroform through his nostrils until he was quiet. I'd made some mistakes with the dosage in the past, however, through trial and error; I had just about mastered the amount needed to bring a project back to my basement without incident.

Ah yes, here it is, genitalia. I flipped through a few pages until I found the diagram I had been searching for. I wasn't an expert on anatomy, and by no means a doctor, but I tried to learn, and to retain as much information as possible from each session. I also made an effort to avoid premature death so that the project could be fully cleansed of their sins before I sent them to the next phase of life, whatever that may be.

It was true that I did not believe in a higher power, however, I did believe in the will of the universe, action and reaction. My justification for torture was a reaction to Jeb's actions. I fantasized that what I was doing was simply letting nature take its course… in the name of a righteous cause that I still have not named. The purpose of that was not to mask regret, or push me over the threshold of fear, as I experienced neither while I was working. It was to be poetic.

After slowly examining the tools before me I decided that the nail clippers would be used first on his penis. I would see if it was possible to amputate the head without assistance from other tools. Before I began I poured more bleach onto his genitals, as they reeked of his ailments. I removed the latex gloves I'd been using and put on large chemical gloves, a surgical mask, and a long rubber apron that I kept stored in the janitorial bin to my left.

Jeb's rapidly blinking eyes followed me closely, fearfully, as I lifted his penis upwards with pliers. I showed him the fingernail clippers so that he was absolutely aware of what I was about to do to him. He squealed and squirmed about but it was useless. I was in control. The first clip took more effort than I had anticipated. I had to tug at the instrument to break the skin away. His body writhed in agony as I worked.

After about twenty minutes I had successfully removed the penis head. I held it up closely to Jeb's eyes and let him see what I had done to him. Tears of terror rolled down the sides of his face as he hyperventilated from the shock. I placed the flesh onto a metal tray next to my instruments and dropped the clippers into a bucket of bleach water.

His crimes were vast... but the crimes I was concerned with the most were his sexual assaults. It was important for him to feel pain in the areas that he once drew pleasure from. The testicles would be next and I would need a face shield for that.

After hammering nails through the thin flesh of his sack to keep everything in place, I grabbed the rubber mallet I had used earlier to silence his muffled screams. I raised it high, theatrically, so that he knew what was coming. After a few practice swings to build the anticipation, just barely brushing the flesh as I did, he shut his eyes and began to cry like a child. That would not suffice. I shouted his name to grab his attention, and as I did his eyes opened. I knew I didn't have much time before he shut them again. Quickly I slammed the mallet down onto the testicle I was aiming for. It flattened out and the skin cracked open, shooting blood against his thighs. Jeb whaled in agony but no mercy would be shown. I immediately crushed the other testicle and then proceeded to beat the top of his thighs and abdomen until sweat fell from the bottom edge of my face shield and lactic acid commanded my arm to stop.

His long, crusted yellow toenails became the next focus of my attention. After driving nails through the knuckle of each toe, and into a board that I'd screwed into the bottom of his feet, I began the next phase. Using a tack-hammer and a small chisel, I started at the tip of the nail plates, wedging the sharp chamfered edge in-between the soft flesh and the nail. One has to be very attentive to the procedure or the nails can be lost. Once I'd lifted the nails all the way back to their roots, which kept them attached, I dripped sulfuric acid onto the tender, exposed flesh. Jeb fought consciousness from the pain, but there was no need to be alarmed; he would be fully coherent soon, returning back to the nightmare he had created for himself.

Next would be the anal cavity. I studied Vlad the Impeller extensively and would be borrowing his technique; however, some slight modifications were required. I could not undo the leather straps that contained Jeb. It was too risky. I also decided against a full impalement as it would likely have killed him before I was finished with my work.

I'd taken the wooden closet-pole I had purchased from the hardware store and carefully sharpened and sanded the insertion end for easier entry into the body. I dipped it into a bucket of used motor oil and made sure that a minimum of sixteen inches was fully covered in the black sludge. It was ready to be inserted into Jeb's body.

That was the first time I had tried to impale through the anal cavity and had some difficulty doing it. I couldn't move Jeb's legs any further apart than they already were, and flipping him over would take too much time, as I would have to use more chloroform and then unstrap him. There would also be a chance of escape, and I simply could not take that risk. I would have to force it in as far as possible by hand and then hammer it the rest of the way.

I explained to Jeb what I was about to do to him, sparing no details as I did. Mucus bubbles and saliva bursts out from his flaring nostrils as I spoke and his smothered screams vibrated the table he was strapped to. I imagined that his sexually assaulted victims responded in similar fashion.

It was much more difficult to impale than I had pictured. It had taken me ten minutes to push in the tip roughly ten inches. I simply could not get it to go any further with just my hands. The hammer I was using was made for forming heavy metals. The head alone weighed threes pounds and would supply enough impact to get the job done.

After the first blow to the closet pole, Jeb's torso jerked up and down off of the table in protest. Hatred consumed me, as he was still denying that he deserved his punishment. Losing control, I smashed the end of the pole over and over, inching it into his body until the oil soaked portion of the wood was no longer visible. I knew that I had ruptured his entrails and that the internal bleeding had begun. My time with Jeb was very limited and I had to hurry to the next phase.

I approached the vise that was holding his head in place and give it a quarter turn. I wanted to make sure I had his attention. I lowered myself down to his right ear and explained to him that I was going to cut off his lips, and his tongue. Before beginning I used the remote on my instrument table to turn the volume of the stereo all the way up. Though the basement had been sound proofed with multiple layers of foam and insulation, I wanted to make sure that if any noise escaped to the outside world it could easily be washed out by the sounds of Pearl Jam's excellent piece of work "Jeremy". I did not know the names of Jeb's victims, but I felt that that song best described a child in pain, a child who had been abused and was ultimately unable to cope with it.

After removing the dirty socks from his mouth he begged me to stop, to call an ambulance… to show mercy. That only fueled my rage further. He battled the speculum as I put it into his mouth and stretched his jaws open as far as the tool would torque them. Taking his lips, one at a time in the pliers; I began to saw away at them with the survival knife taken from my instrument table. His agony was nearly drowned out by the wonderful music, but enough pain could be heard to derive pleasure from. Once that process was completed I moved on to his tongue. He tried to pull it away, as if he could hide it in the back of his throat, but it was no match for the clamping force of the pliers. I ripped his tongue outward with great force and cut it off slowly. He gurgled and choked on the blood, his body convulsing as he did.

After placing the removed items onto the metal tray, I stood back and examined my work. I looked into his eyes and asked him how he was feeling. He could only reply with guttural garble. I was hoping for more, but I had taken away most of his ability to communicate.

It was time to finish it. It was important that Jeb die directly by my hands, and not from the bleeding. After dumping his tongue, his lips, and the head of his wart littered penis into his mouth, I removed the speculum and taped it shut. I then turned the vice slowly, and as I did his body flailed about in seizures. Bubbling fluids and streams of blood seeped out of the cracks where his broken skull has severed the flesh. A few moments later Jeb's last breath left his nostrils. He was dead. He had been baptized for his sins.

Chapter 13: Climax

With Jebediah out of the way I could concentrate solely on Linda. There was only fifteen minutes left until I needed to leave my house and pick her up for our date. On the telephone we had discussed possibilities for the location. I took command of the conversation and told her that it would be a surprise. I knew that would show her that I was a man who was not afraid to take control of the situation, and that I had a romantic side to me. Most importantly, the thought of surprise would keep me on her mind and provide a shroud of mystery. From what I'd been reading mystery was a crucial element in the world of romance. Women who were kept on their toes felt that they were in an exciting relationship and would be much less likely to lose interest.

We had reservations and would be attending an expensive comedy club that served food and alcohol. We would have one hour and fifteen minutes to order, eat, talk, and enjoy our drinks. The performers would then come on stage for one hour of standup comedy. After that I would gauge her reaction and body language. If she still appeared vibrant, I would take her to the nearby beach where we would stroll on the boardwalk and take part in any activities that she may fancy. If not, I would take her home, or anywhere that she requested, and have to improvise from there.

All of the prep work had been completed. I scrubbed every inch of my body twice with expensive soap, shaved and trimmed much of my body hair, ironed my clothes, and rehearsed for many hours in the mirror. Everything was perfect, to include my new vehicle.

Initially I was displeased with my former car being totaled, but eventually saw an opportunity to gain from it. My new truck had an aggressive look on the exterior, but had a refined quality on the interior. I also added an aftermarket muffler to enhance the sound of the large V-8 engine. It wasn't obnoxiously loud, but the illusion of additional power had been added. The vehicle better suited the new persona that I had mastered and I believed that Linda would enjoy it.

Before leaving the house I took one final look in the mirror, inspecting every cavity and opening on my head. Everything was clean and in order, I was ready. With a final brush through my slicked back hair I walked out of the bathroom and headed out to my truck.

As I pulled into Linda's driveway I began to feel nervous, an emotion that had not occurred many times in the past. I would remain calm and stick to the game plan. If my studies were correct, she would be equally nervous and willing to overlook any minor lapses in judgment on my part. I would use her awkwardness to my advantage by not acknowledging it. No matter what she said, or how many times she fumbled her words, I would keep pushing forward.

The doorbell light had lost its glow. I knocked. After three moderate swings of the antique door-knocker I stood and waited. Linda's mother opened the door to my surprise. She looked to be in her early sixties. Her hair was short and thinning on top, but was well kept, and her face was attractive for her age. She walked with a cane and wore a shawl upon her back. A very old necklace, Rosary beads, rested between her sagging breasts.

"Hi there, you must be John?" Her voice was kind and her face glowed happily as she awaited my reply. "Yes ma'am, I'm here to pick up Linda for our date."

"Oh, that is so sweet; you are just as handsome as Linda told me you were."

"Mom…" Linda looked embarrassed as she approached her mother from behind, kissing her on the cheek and heading out the door to stand next to me.

"I need to get to bed, church in the morning… You two have fun." The two women hugged and Linda's mother told me that she was glad to meet me, and that she hoped to see me again soon. That was a good sign.

After her mother closed the door Linda apologized to me out of embarrassment. I told her not to worry about it, and that her mother reminded me of my own. That seemed to comfort her and ease the initial tension that we were both experiencing, but that I refused to show.

I'd chosen the music for our journey carefully. Should our conversation come to a halt for any reason, the classic sounds of nineties pop-country would provide a distraction and promote feelings of well-being and contentment. I'd downloaded over thirty songs that were in the top twenty charts for the decade and added them to the mp3 player that came with the truck. There was a mixture of male and female vocalist to show that I respected both walks of life equally. I also avoided all slow, sad, and romantic tracks. Every song was based around having a good time, and I believed that would have a positive effect on her consciousness. It would help relieve any pressure she had placed upon herself. It also suggested that I was very easy going, and that our night would be filled with fun.

"So, is where you are taking me still a surprise?"
I responded with a flirtatious smile, making as much eye contact that was safely possible while driving.

"It is, and I think you are going to really enjoy it. Tonight is going to be fun, I promise."

As we drove along, making small talk and laughing at nothing in particular, Linda caught me off guard. A move took place that I did not anticipate, that I was not prepared for. She proclaimed "Oh my God! I love this song! I haven't heard it in ages!" She then took off her seatbelt and slid over next to me, singing every word perfectly in tune with the song. I kept glancing down but she was not even attempting to buckle the lap belt that was provided for the center seat. A rush of heat warmed my insides as the anxiety set in. I couldn't possibly request for her to put it on, it was much too soon for that, much too forward. However, losing her in an accident... having her fly through the windshield... That was something that must be avoided... She couldn't end up like Sophia.

Relief washed over me. After the first few versus of the song were completed, Linda buckled the belt as she cutely bobbed her head about to the music. I did not want to interrupt her, and she didn't seem to want to talk right then. She made eyes at me from time to time, but kept on singing until the song was over. She giggled and kissed me on the cheek. The tension had melted away and for the rest of the trip we sat side by side chit-chatting, listening to the music and enjoying the ride.

Most of the people who were sitting in the dining area of the comedy club with us were in their late twenties and early thirties. Like us, they were dressed in nice, but casual clothing. We fit in perfectly among the other dates and I could tell that Linda loved my surprise.

After enjoying our meal and engaging in small talk, she sipped at her wine while I enjoyed my cranberry juice. I didn't want to tell her that I no longer drink alcohol, as that could make her suspicious. I told her that since I was driving I didn't want to drink, but I would take a rain check. She was content with my response.

There were four comedians, and the first three performers were what I would consider to be good, clean comics. They had the half drunken crowd roaring with laughter, to include Linda, and I played along with them as the punch lines landed. After the third comic left the stage the man who had introduced them all came back and told us that he had a surprise guest for us.

"That's right ladies and gents… you may recognize our next comic from his many appearances on television and his smash hit comedy special… Give the man a warm welcome… Barney Lopez!"

The crowd erupted with excitement, many people standing as they clapped and cheered. I'd never heard of the man but Linda was ecstatic by the news. A skinny Spanish man with buckteeth and crazy, wide open eyes ran onto the stage, taking the microphone from the MC who gave the introduction. He screamed out with a goofy, high pitched voice "What's up New Jersey?! I'm glad to be back in my home state!" The people again howled and clapped wildly before settling down.

Barney paced back and forth across the stage, engaging audience members as he did. He made fun of their clothing, their hair, their weight… everything. His jokes became more and more vulgar as he moved from person to person. My intuition told me that we would be victims of his verbal assault, and I was correct.

Linda was among the most beautiful women in the crowd. Barney stopped and stared at her. "God damn! Now that is a fine piece of pussy right there! Tell me sweetie… Please! Tell me that your man is hittin that right!" Linda looked at me nervously, and then back at Barney, and replied with a sassy tone "If he wasn't I wouldn't be here with him."

The females in the crowd cheered and a large black woman came over and gave her a high-five. I remained calm, objective, forcing a smile and a head nod at the comedian. I was hoping that he would move on, but he turned his attention to me.

"Look at this motha fucka, straight out of the nineteen fifties! Tell me man, how much motor oil do you have to use to keep your hair looking like that?" I ignored him as he continued. "Well, if your lady ever gets the urge to do anal, you can just swipe some of that hair grease on your dick and slide right in!"

The people around us chuckled and hollered as my hateful gaze forced Barney's eyes away from my own, making him uncomfortable enough to move on with the show. It was too early to tell, but I believed that Linda was disappointed that I did not play along. I'd figure out a way to smooth it out once we left that place.

After Barney left the stage, the crowd began to dwindle. Linda finished her glass of wine and told me that she needed to use the restroom before we left. As she walked away, Barney caught my eye from the side of the stage. He was laughing and pointing at me with the other comedians. The rage that I had been able to control in recent months was too much to handle. I had to hurt him.

I left one hundred dollars on the table, leaving a tip of forty dollars, and followed the comedian as he walked out of the rear exit with a cigarette in his hand. He was alone and no one appeared to be paying attention. Unaware that I was standing behind him, he lit the cigarette and started puffing away as he fumbled with his cell phone. That was my chance. I punched him as hard as I could with a right hook, landing cleanly on his lower jaw. As expected, he fell face first onto the asphalt and began to snore as his nervous system adjusted to the impact. I dragged him over to the dumpster and hoisted him inside, covering him with trash and punching him in the face several more times before closing the lid. I then walked back into the building and sat down at the table as if I'd never left. I didn't give the club my real name when I made the reservations and I had paid with cash. That should have protected me from discovery...fuck... I hadn't considered the possibility of cameras. I scanned the room carefully and saw none. I had to be more careful. Linda was changing me. I could no longer act on impulse to protect her honor; I would have to make better decisions in the future.

I sat patiently sipping my cranberry juice. As Linda came out of the restroom I walked toward her and when we were close enough she asked me if I was ready to leave. I smiled innocently and said "sure".

The two glasses of wine that Linda had drank had her very loose and talkative. She told me about her childhood, her mother, how funny the first three comedians were... anything and everything she could think of. I tried to pay close attention so that I could respond appropriately and exploit any openings that may present themselves, but it had begun to rain and I didn't want to get into another accident.

"So, John, where are we going next?"

Linda playfully rubbed my bicep as she snuggled closer. I responded

"Well, I had planned to take you down to the boardwalk, but it looks like the rain is picking up, I'd hate to take you home to your mother soaking wet. She became excited at the thought.

"How romantic would that be? We could skip the boardwalk and stroll along the beach in the summer rain... It almost sounds like a movie… Let's do it! The rain isn't that bad, we'll be alright."

The thought of mildew growing on my wet interior over night was not pleasing, but much of the reason I'd bought the new truck was to please Linda. She came first, I would contend with the stink of mildew in the morning. I agreed with her, that it would be romantic, and that we'd head to the beach.

As we walked along the beach hand in hand, not a soul could be seen. The rain and the darkness had driven them all away. Linda's makeup was slightly running along the sides of her face, but it only made me more attracted to her. She wasn't insecure about her appearance. She didn't mind if I saw her when she wasn't at her best. Linda knew that I too was in love, and that all of the formalities, the dancing shyly around touchy subjects… it was no longer necessary. Either that, or the alcohol was still in her bloodstream and her inhibitions had not yet returned. That was most likely the case.

"John…"

She said it sweetly while tugging at my hand, signaling that she wanted me to stop walking. I turned and faced her. Looking into her eyes I waited for her to continue. She studied me peacefully for a few moments, pulling me closer, and then began kissing me lustfully, rubbing and massaging my back as she did. As each second passed she became more sexual in her actions, moving her mouth down to my neck and pulling upward on my shirt so that she could slide it off.

I was hesitant, as I did not want to have the awkward conversations over the next few weeks about how she was intoxicated and how it was a mistake, but I could not resist. She smelled so clean, so womanly.

She continued on. Moving down to my jeans, she kissed my stomach as she fondled me, slowly unbuttoning, and then unzipping me. My heart was racing as she pulled my manhood from my briefs and slid it into her mouth. It wasn't like the dirty animals I had all of my sexual experiences with. I was sober, my blood flow was strong, and I cared for Linda.

I tried to conceal it, but I knew Linda could hear me gasping for air as her head moved back and forth, her tongue passionately licking, her mouth gently sucking at my flesh. It was wonderful.

No thoughts of the universe or its practical functionality entered my mind. I was able to fully focus on the current activity and enjoy it.

As she licked and sucked I was coming closer to orgasm and she wasn't slowing down. I started to panic. I did not want to cum in her mouth, as it was something we had not discussed. Nor had I ever rehearsed warning a woman, or even read about it. I didn't want to sound pathetic, but I also didn't want to offend her. The more I thought about it the closer I was, and the more I tried to stop it, the better it felt.

My knees quivered as I came into Linda's mouth. I stood silently watching my love, waiting to see what would happen. She showed no sign of discomfort or disgust. She slowed down, eventually coming to a stop. As she looked up at me, a smile formed across her beautiful face. She had swallowed it.

Linda pulled me down to my knees next to her and then removed her summer dress. Though it was dark I could still make out her beautiful body under the polluted New Jersey sky. She had on a small bra, and to my delight, no panties. She was stunning.

"Here, we'll lay on this."

She pointed to her dress, and spread it out like a blanket. After removing her bra she laid on her back and I hovered above her, appreciating her beauty. I then did as she had done to me; kissing her soft neck, massaging her breasts and gently pulling at her nipples as I worked my way down.

I rubbed the hood of her sensitive clit lightly, letting my instincts lead the way, but staying mindful of the articles I'd read on oral sex. Her breath quickened as my lips kissed and pulled gently at her labia. I then slid one finger slowly inside of her, letting it become fully lubricated before using any real force.

She gasped and grabbed the back of my head as I licked her clit and moved the two middle fingers of my right hand in and out of her, applying upward pressure to the spongy area just inside her vagina, stimulating her g-spot.

I let her body and the pressure from her hands dictate the pace of the action. The faster she inhaled, the faster my fingers slid in and out of her. She began to moan as quick breaths passed her lips, and then, she began to buck and squirm wildly. I quickened my strokes, and as I did, the walls of her moist vagina closed in on my fingers. She was cumming; I had succeeded.

After the initial tightening of her vaginal muscles, I slowed my pace and avoided any direct contact with the clitoris itself. I calmly and gently rubbed the outer folds of her labia and waited for her response.

Linda eventually came back to reality and pulled me up toward her, hugging my torso tightly and softly kissing my lips. The unique mixture of our bodies tasted wonderful. I couldn't think of anything to say, as the last twenty minutes had me in a daze.

She playfully pushed me onto my back and then cuddled up close, resting her head on my chest and squeezing me. As we lay there, staring up at the foggy half-moon, I felt content and at peace. I had nothing to analyze or hate. We were simply two animals who would rely on each other from that point on.

Neither of us spoke on the ride back to Linda's house. She sat as close as she could to me, holding my arm and resting her head on my shoulder. At every point where her body touched my own I received pleasant chills, like electricity sparking between our flesh. I had to keep it going. Linda would be my wife, and I would do anything to make it happen.

As we stood on her front porch she held onto my shoulders and asked me "When will I see you again, John?"

With an easy smile I replied "Soon. I have another surprise ready for you, and I think you are going to love it."

She blew me a kiss as I drove away.

Chapter 14: Exude

The first date with Linda had gone well and we were set up again to go out; however I still had three days until I had to pick her up. I had told her it would be a surprise, but I still wasn't sure what we were going to do.

I called in sick on Wednesday and went out for a long drive in my truck to come up with a solution. As the cars passed me by on the freeway I looked at every business sign that I passed, but nothing was standing out. I wanted it to be fun for her, but intimate at the same time.

I decided stop at a diner to give my head a break. The building looked to have been built in the fifties or sixties and the sign out front was only four or five feet tall. As I entered the diner I was greeted by a young geeky looking kid with glasses and a face wrecked with pimples. He asked me how many, and after telling him that I would be eating alone he sat me down at a table back in the corner.

There were only a few elderly people sitting around and I was glad, I needed to relax. Not long after the geeky kid walked away a young girl, probably in her early twenties, came up to me and gleefully said "Hi there and welcome to Joe's. Can I get you anything to drink?" I'd thought about getting a coffee seeing as Linda loved the stuff, but I just hadn't been able to develop a taste for it.

"I'll just have some water please."

With that the waitress whose name tag red "Carline" walked away at a brisk pace. I scanned over the menu, looking for something healthy and decided to go with plain oatmeal and a vegie-omelet.

After Carline took my order I stared into my glass of ice water and began thinking about Linda again. I was so infatuated with her that it felt painful. I supposed that is what the poets of old wrote about; that yearning feeling and fear of failure. Hmm, failure… That wasn't a pleasant thought. However, I had to be realistic about the situation. I was living a lie. Though the persona I had adopted from Mr. Dean was working well, and was automatic, it truly wasn't me. If I was to ever slip, to show my true nature, the violent animal that I was, Linda would not be able to handle it.

The food was decent. After finishing up Carline brought me the check. When I went to see how much I owed I saw that she had written her phone number down with a smiley face next to it. It was amazing how much different my life had become since I started taking care of myself. However, I would throw the number out the window as soon as I got back on the road. Leaving that in a pocket or lying around my truck would only hurt Linda if she saw it, even though I would be innocent of temptation.

As I continued my drive down the long stretch of highway something finally caught my eye. A sign reaching high into the sky read "House of Blues." That would be perfect to start things off.

I went inside to inspect the place and was pleased with the quality. It had a vintage feel to it, the kind of place where legends played. All along the wooden walls there were autographed photos of B.B. King, Stevie Ray Vaughan, and a plethora of others. All types of guitars and blues memorabilia sat in glass cases with descriptions next to them. The place was legit. It would offer live entertainment and keep the level of excitement in the relationship high.

Except for a few drunks sitting at the bar the place was empty, as it looked to be mostly a night club. I went and took a seat at the bar and not long after a short, southern talking black man came out of the back doors.

"Hey, my man, what can I get for you? We got every beer under the sun on tap…"

"Hey, how's it going? I just stopped in to see when the next live band would be playing, and do you offer reservations?"

"Sorry boss, we don't offer no reservations. On the flip side, there is gonna be a good local talent passing through on Saturday night. Here's a flyer for it if you wanna take it with you."

I thanked the man and headed back to my house. There was still planning to do and I needed to do more research on the blues just in case Linda had any questions on the subject.

Back at my house I went straight to my room and hopped on the computer. I scrolled through the history of blues music, and read the biographies of all the greats. I listened to samples of the band that would be playing on Saturday. It was a bit rowdy for my taste but it sounded like it would create the right type of atmosphere I was looking for.

As I read through the biography of B.B. King and saw the title of a song he had taken part in "Blues Hotel", it hit me. Linda had said on the phone that she wanted to finish what we'd started, and I did as well. But, I was not ready for her to come to my home yet. I still needed to do some redecorating and buy a new bed. A very high level, expensive hotel room would be the best option.

After looking around on the internet for an hour or so I ended up finding one near the top floor of a Hotel. It was eight hundred dollars a night and looked more like a massive studio apartment than a hotel room. Everything was brand new, there was a full bar, a circular bed, and a large hot tub in the center of the room. The view was also quite good by the looks of the photograph. It was almost perfect. The only downside is that it was a thirty minute ride from the blues club, and sat in the heart of Atlantic City. However, Linda would likely enjoy a few drinks and would be in good spirits for the ride.

I knew that Linda didn't have a lot of money. She was in debt with her student loans and only made a small income from the coffee shop. To give her the better things in life would further solidify my standing as an alpha male, a man who could take care of her and make her happy. I had to be careful though. If she became too accustomed to the expensive lifestyle I would end up letting her down in the future. I would have to lie as to how I acquired the room. I would tell her that a friend from work had a time share and that he gave me a good deal on it. Though I'd saved up thirty thousand dollars over the past few years, it would dwindle quickly if I wasn't careful.

After meeting Linda's mother again, who was very happy to see me, we headed out toward the blues club. The entire ride over Linda was kissing me and rubbing my chest, my thighs, and my cock. I had to focus on the task at hand and tune out her pleasant touch or I wouldn't be able to leave the vehicle once we stopped. We would have to sit awkwardly for a few minutes until my hard-on had died down.

We got to the club a little late and the band had already started playing. Unfortunately there were no tables left and we had to grab a seat at the bar. Linda didn't seem to mind as she shouted to the bartender for a light beer and then asked me what I wanted. I hesitated. I did not want to use the sober driver excuse again. I didn't want to seem lame, like I couldn't cut loose and get a little reckless. I thought to myself *Fuck it*, for Linda, I will order a double of Whisky. I will drink it straight like the old pro that I am, no weakling facial expressions, just a slight smile of enjoyment.

"I'll take a double of whisky and let's go ahead and open up a tab."

The friendly southern sounding black bartender I'd met a few days prior smiled big and replied:

"Hey! No problem my man! Good to see you back here; one beer and one double whiskey coming right up!"

I took down the shot with ease and felt that Linda was impressed by my fortitude. I wasn't happy about drinking the whisky but it was a necessary evil for the relationship to stay healthy. Within two or three minutes I could feel the alcohol doing its work. I hadn't drank in months and my body had been fully clean until that moment. It felt good. I had a certain level of aggression that I hadn't felt in a while, and though it had to stay hidden, I enjoyed the surge of power it gave me. It also helped me to loosen up, and become more flirtatious with Linda.

She went through two beers in the next twenty minutes or so and started to get a little wild as the music blared all around us. She would dance between my legs and tug at my lower lip with her own. The two hundred or so people around us were so loud and rowdy that I don't think they noticed, and if they did, they didn't give a shit about what we were doing.

"Hey! I'm gonna run to the ladies room real fast. I'll be right back!"

As she walked away in her heals I admired her beautiful legs and ass. She was wearing some sort of jean skirt outfit and jacket. I didn't know much about female clothing but Linda looked gorgeous in it.

After ten minutes passed I became concerned. Surely the line wasn't that long. I told the friendly bartender I would be right back and headed around the corner to see if she was still waiting in line for the restroom.

There was a drunken man, a typical meathead-looking jerkoff blocking Linda's path with his hand that was placed on the wall beside her shoulder. She was looking around nervously and then found my eyes. She opened them wide, showing her relief. I walked faster and as Linda continued to look in my direction the asshole turned his head toward me. I spoke before he had a chance.

"Excuse me, sir, my lady-friend and I need to head out, sorry for the interruption but we have somewhere we have to be."

I Grabbed Linda's hand and pulled her toward me, and as I did he dropped his hand from the wall and turned to face me.

"Hey, fuck-face! Do you know who I am?" He growled drunkenly as he spoke, a form of communication I was all too familiar with. I replied simply "No."

He finished the bottle of beer in his hand and then spoke again, that time with more aggression as he stepped closer.

"We weren't finished with our conversation yet. Why don't you go back over to the bar like a good bitch and I'll send her over when I'm finished..."

I ignored his bait and put my body between Linda and the drunken idiot, giving her a small nudge on her lower back to walk forward. We didn't make it but two or three steps and the unmistakable thud of a beer bottle that refused to break hit me in the back of the head. Linda screamed, and as she did I could see the bouncers making their way through the crowd toward us.

I had wanted to avoid any form of violence or macho behavior in front of Linda, as I had read multiple times women did not find that attractive. However, that man's disrespect had gone too far. He had made Linda uncomfortable, and he had openly challenged me. I had to punish him.

I pushed Linda further away, as gently as I could considering the circumstances and turned around to face the man who was standing in his best Irish fighting stance, yelling and taunting me.

"Come on you fuckin faggot, let's see if I can make that pretty hair of yours bounce around a little more…"

The whisky, the rage, I let it possess me, as it would guide me through the situation without further thought. He jabbed at me with his lead hand, and as he did I slipped to the side and punched him in the throat with a textbook overhand right. He dropped to his knees instantly, gripping his neck and gasping for air. I then followed up with a soccer kick to the side of his head, my boot landing cleanly on his lower jaw. He crashed into the wall face first and then slid down, blood seeping from his unconscious mouth as he did.

The bouncers arrived and put distance between the defeated foe and myself. I remained calm and patient as one of them spoke.

"We saw him attack you first, it looked like self-defense… I'm an off duty police officer, do you need an ambulance?"

"No, that's alright. I'm not hurt too bad, just a little shaken up… He might need one though."

"Are you sure, it won't take long…"

"I'm fine, is it alright if we leave?"

"Hang tight, we need to ask you and the lady here a few questions."

After the off duty police officer got the full story from Linda, how the drunken man wouldn't let her out of the hallway, and how he had clearly attacked me first, as the security footage proved, and as they had witnessed, they had us sign a statement and freed us to leave after I insisted on not pressing charges.

I closed out my tab and we headed out into the parking lot toward my truck. Linda rubbed my back as we walked and asked me if I was ok over and over. I responded as coolly as I could, not wanting to overdo the tough guy routine. I told her that I had a little bit of a headache, but that I had had worse.

Wanting to lighten up the mood I put some fifties rock on the truck stereo, but it didn't seem to comfort Linda. She sat next to me quietly looking straight ahead. I wasn't sure what to do, or where she was emotionally, so I also sat quietly, trying to make my expression as pleasant as possible. As I had anticipated, she spoke first.

"John… that was scary…"

"Yes, it was, I didn't expect something like that to happen." I laughed a little, trying to cheer her up.

"When he hit you with the bottle… your facial expression… it was terrifying… like a monster… and then you just… it was like a movie… I'm sorry, John, I'm just shaken up from it all… Thank you for protecting me."

She leaned in and kissed me on the cheek before resting her head on my shoulder. She remained quiet until the lights of Atlantic City came into view.

"I had been so lost in thought I just assumed we were going home…"

"I still have one more surprise for you. I think you are really going to love it."

Linda's smile reached from ear to ear as we pulled into the parking garage of the hotel. I gave the desk my information and received the key to our room. The elevator ride was long, and Linda became more excited as we rose higher and higher. Finally, the ding sound came we had been waiting for.

After a short stroll down the hall we found our room. I let Linda enter first before turning on the light switch. Her hands flew up toward her mouth as she gasped.

"Oh my God... This is so... incredible! How did you get this?"

"I thought you'd enjoy it... A friend from work helped me out... It's been a stressful night, what do you say we have a few glasses of champagne and relax in the hot tub?"

Linda rubbed her hand down my chest and said in a sultry voice:

"Let me... freshen up. I expect you to be naked when I come back."

As she walked away I headed over to the bar and found the most expensive looking bottle of champagne I could find. After grabbing two glasses I went back over to the hot tub, removed all of my clothing and hopped in. The water was still room temperature but after I hit the on switch it heated up quickly and bubbles covered the top of the water.

Linda came out of the restroom with a fancy looking robe on. The kind of robe the hotel only provided for rich guests. She dimmed the lights and headed over toward me, stopping just as she reached the steps leading into the comforting water. Her expression was one of a woman who was ready to be naughty as she untied the cotton belt from around her waist and let the robe slide off of her shoulders and onto the tile floor.

That was the first time I saw her naked body in a decently lit environment. Though the lights had been dimmed, I was still able to appreciate every inch of her and found no flaws. As she walked up the steps her firm breast jiggled slightly. Her pubic hair had been cleanly removed and I could see her outer labia softly slide against her inner thighs as she took each step.

Linda waded over to where I was sitting and sat on my lap, surely feeling my rock hard cock rubbing against her thigh. I poured us each half a glass from the champagne bottle and playfully toasted to a wild night. I sipped at the drink and

Linda knocked hers back like it was a shot of whisky. After setting the glasses off to the side she began kissing me. Her tongue darted around in my mouth passionately as I caressed her perfect body. She whispered in my ear, a hint of sexual aggression in her voice:

"John... I want you inside of me…"

Before I could respond she took control of the situation. She turned her back to me and put my throbbing cock inside of her. She was incredibly tight, and her insides were warm and inviting. After she slid down the shaft, all the way to the hilt, she gasped with pleasure and quickened her pace. I grabbed her breast and stabilized her body as she moved her ass up and down, pounding against me with great intensity.

That went on for a few minutes, and then she began to orgasm, and as she did she said the dirty words I wasn't expecting, but was glad to hear:

"Cum inside of me… I want to feel you…"

I may have been able to hold out for a while longer, but Linda asking for my seed, saying it as if she needed it, was too much to handle. Moments later I exploded inside of her, gripping her tightly as I did and forcing myself all the way in.

We made love several more times as the night passed, kissing, licking, and sucking every part of each other's body. It was perfect. The night had started off rough, and I wasn't sure I would be able to pull it off, but it came to fruition. The more I thought about it, the more I realized that the violence that had taken place at the blues bar had excited Linda. Though she had been scared, it gave her a primal charge. The danger, the fighting, the craziness of it all removed her from her boring life of school and taking care of her mother.

Chapter 15: Pharmaceutical

As the months went on Linda and I became closer. However, my urges had begun to resurface and grew stronger by the day, an issue that had to be dealt with. Making love to her often had greatly reduced the temptation to kill. Yet, the more contact I had with Linda, the more accustomed to it I became. It was still a thrilling experience each time, but it was starting to not be enough.

Alcohol was out of the question. I would only drink when Linda did and that was that. I didn't want to get caught up in my previous lifestyle, as the discipline I had maintained had allowed me to have what I wanted most and I didn't want to jeopardize it. I needed to find something new to take its place or I would soon be selecting another project to dissect.

I had spent weeks on the internet studying legal pharmaceuticals that I could get my hands on with the right list of ailments. Pain killers, anti-depressants, and shit they give to kids to keep them calm; I considered all of it. However, the side effects for each product would take too much away from my sexual function and the intensity required to keep my body in top form.

I then came across an article on medical marijuana. The more I read into it, the more interested I became. I watched videos of cancer patients, those stricken with AIDs, fibromyalgia, muscular dystrophy, and a laundry list of other diseases. Their state of wellbeing was clearly visible, and it was due to the marijuana. There were also videos of professional fighters and various other types of athletes who used marijuana as not only a way to help with pain, but to help them focus during their training. They claimed that it elevated them, that they had reached new heights and understandings in their respected sports, places that would not be possible without the help of THC.

I found no side effects other than increased metabolism, sleepiness, and the possibility of anxiety and panic attacks if too much was consumed. There were no reported cases of cancer, emphysema, or lung disease being directly linked to the drug. Not a single death had yet been linked to marijuana. I was impressed, and the more I read, the more perplexed I became about why it was illegal. I supposed the rich old crows that supported the politicians still saw it as a mind killer from the hippie generation.

As I went down the list of ailments required in the state of New Jersey to obtain medicinal marijuana, it was clear that I had none of them, and I would not be able to fake it under a doctor's keen eye. I also had another problem on my hands. Though medical marijuana had recently been legalized in New Jersey, I was still a federal employee, and under federal law, marijuana, even if prescribed by a doctor, was still illegal. I received random drug tests once or twice a year at the job and couldn't afford to be caught using it. That could destroy everything with Linda.

After extensive research I found a "head shop" that was out of state, but only a short drive. In four hours I had reached the store in Maryland. As I examined their wares I came across the item that I'd been looking for. It would be my saving grace if I was to be drug tested. It was a fake penis with an I.V. bag attached to it. It could easily be strapped to the thigh.

I already had four gallons of frozen urine in my freezer. I would simply need to thaw it out, and then slowly heat it to ninety-eight-point-six degrees before putting it in the bag.

After leaving the store I headed back home. I stopped for gas, and when I did the plastic bag containing the fake penis blew open. The clerk had given me the black version. That would not suffice, as a noncommissioned officer or fresh lieutenant had to see the urine leave the penis and enter the cup when being drug tested. I had already driven three hours and was almost home but I had to fix the problem.

Driving along the highway I saw a sign that read "XXX Adult Store". I took the exit that was on the sign and pulled up into the parking lot. The inside of the establishment was grimy. There were thousands of DVDs, a massive rack of magazines, and posters everywhere. However, I did not see any sex toys.

I approached the cashier. He was a scrawny looking guy with dead eyes. Tattoos covered both of his arms and neck. He also had a metal stud through the bridge of his nose that looked like a cock.

"Excuse me, do you sell dildos here?" He didn't seem disturbed at all by my question, which I suppose was to be expected.

"Yeah man, they are in the back room over there. Are you looking for anything in particular?"

"I need it to be less than six inches in length and it has to match my skin tone."

"No problem, I think I have just the thing for you. Follow me."

I followed the man through the anal sex DVD section and into the back room. It was like a temple. There were hundreds of dildos, rubber vaginas, blow up dolls, beads, and all sorts of sex toys stacked from the floor to the ceiling against every wall. It was impressive.

Between the stacks of boxes there were two black doors with sliders on them that read "occupied". The clerk noticed me staring at them and told me "Those guys shouldn't be much longer. If you want to check out some vids and jerk off a little bit you can do it in there... And don't worry, we run a legit operation here. I personally clean every room after every use." He stood proudly, awaiting my response.

"No thanks, I don't have much time today…"

He shrugged and then went on looking for the item I had requested, digging through boxes and looking over an inventory list.

"Here you go man, this looks about your color. It's only four inches long and is really easy on anal entry."

I took the box from him and studied the item. It looked very real and would be passable during a drug test, even under close examination.

"I'll take it."

"Cool man, glad I could help you out… Oh, wait, I almost forgot, its wanker week. All dildos and butt plugs are buy one get one free as long as the secondary item is of equal or lesser value."

I supposed having an extra rubber penis wouldn't hurt if I somehow damaged the original.

"I'll take two of this exact type."

When I got back into the parking lot an idea came to me. Linda and I had been having wonderful sex, or at least that is what she had been telling me, but I sensed that she desired more; something new and daring. In our last encounter I had done as an article suggested and licked the outer area of her anal tissue. She tensed up at first, but soon let herself go. She had really enjoyed it. She would likely be open to more unorthodox methods if it was approached from the right angle.

I left the store with a bag full of dildos, massagers, cock rings, anal beads, and water based lubrication. I wasn't sure how I would bring them up in discussion, or if I would just try to surprise her with them one at a time. I would have to do more research online and see how other couples had brought up the topic before anything.

With the possibility of a drug test taken care of I just needed a way to safely and discreetly get the marijuana.

As I pondered on the subject a magnificent idea presented itself. I would grow it in my basement. YouTube provided me with all of the instructions required to put the grow-cabinet together. I would need soil, pots, aluminum foil, insulation, four florescent lights, a fan, a thermometer and humidity gauge, and a large wooden container. I acquired the items from multiple hardware and gardening stores so that I would not look suspicious.

Then the issue of obtaining seeds presented itself. I bought the cheapest laptop I could find from a local electronics store and took it to a café located about an hour from my house. Once there I used their free wireless internet to search for an online dealer. I found one based out of Canada. After writing down the information needed to order the seeds by mail I left the café and threw the laptop into a small man-made lake along the side of the road.

I ordered the seeds by mailing cash to the company under a fake name and the address of an abandoned house.

The abandoned house was off in the woods about fifteen minutes from my home. I'd discovered it while abducting a dreg a few years back. It was totally isolated, and I would be able to retrieve the mail from the box that was located next to the front door without being seen.

I waited two weeks after the estimated delivery date to retrieve the package. It was two in the morning on a chilly Wednesday night. I parked my truck on a dirt path that led off from the main road near the house. With latex gloves I removed the package from the box and hurried through the woods back to the vehicle. Once inside I stuffed the package inside of a giant bottle of protein powder and buried it at the bottom. I also had exercise clothing and various other supplements in a duffel bag next to the container to reduce any suspicion of wrong doing if I was to be pulled over.

Perhaps I had been a little paranoid about it all, but being paranoid... no, being smart ensures that you will not be caught.

Chapter 16: Sacred Journey

It was mid-December on a Friday night the first time I smoked marijuana.

Linda's mother had flown out to California to visit her dying sister and we had the house all to ourselves. After performing oral sex on her with the help of one of the smaller anal toys I had purchased we laid next to one another cuddling. Though the orgasm had relaxed her temporarily she soon brought up the subject of her final exam that would be taking place Monday morning. She nearly had tears in her eyes as she spoke to me about it.

"John, I have to study for this, I am so nervous… If I don't pass this test I'll have to take the entire course over again…" I consoled her, saying what she needed to hear.

"You'll do great. You work harder than anyone I know… How about this… I'll take care of a few things this weekend that I have been putting off, and that will give you all of Saturday and Sunday to focus on the test. I'll even have lunch and dinner delivered to your door so you don't have to worry about that either."

Linda laughed and cried at the same time, hugging me close and kissing me on the cheek. She then whispered into my ear the words I had been waiting so many months to hear; the words that would lead to our marriage.

"I love you."

I knew that she loved me, and I loved her as well, but neither of us had come out and directly said it yet. I responded with a passionate kiss, and then while looking her in the eyes, told her that I loved her. We cuddled for another half hour before I left. I didn't want to keep her up too late as her passing the course would be important for both of us. If we were to move in together her additional income as a nurse would make our life more enjoyable.

It had been three months since I planted the marijuana. I harvested the buds on the tenth week and had placed them in a jar to dry out a bit as the instructions from the internet said to do.

I headed down into the basement and turned on the stereo. Jimi Hendrix felt appropriate for my adventure. After removing a large bud from the jar and setting it on my workbench I examined it carefully. It was a vibrant green and sticky to the touch. Little red hairs stuck out from all over it and the smell was both powerful and fresh, a smell that I would come to appreciate.

I broke it apart into small pieces and after four attempts was able to roll them correctly into a joint. I had read that smoking for the first time can be a very pleasant experience, or it could be terrifying. The article suggested starting with just one hit, and then, if you felt no effects, take another hit fifteen or twenty minutes later. That is exactly what I did.

The first hit was larger than I had expected. I tried to hold it in for three or four seconds but began coughing uncontrollably. I knew that the plant wasn't responsible for the outburst; it was my improper technique, my inexperience that caused it.

As Jimi played on I could feel a very light tingle throughout my body, a feeling so pleasantly ridiculous that it made me smile uncontrollably. I sat back against the wall and closed my eyes, letting the music decide where my mind went. As the drums and guitar played on, my body felt like it was floating and that the music was circling all around me.

Next, my tongue became numb and my heart rate increased to a rapid pace. That part was not as enjoyable. However, after reading hundreds of other peoples personal experiences I knew that it was normal, and that physically I was in no danger. My mind and body were simply discovering and adapting to the THC. If I tried to fight it I would only force myself into a panic. I had to remind myself that it was impossible for any harm to come to me from the plant, and that the more I relaxed, the more pleasure I would receive.

I began contemplating the structure of the universe. Surely the planet I lived on was not the only floating rock that produced entities. There had to be something more complex. Worlds where there were no rapist, murderers, or molesters, just objective life. Perhaps that is what the animal kingdom on earth was; taking only what one needed to go on. I supposed that, that same thought could be used by a criminal to justify his evil ways, but that would be from a subjective standpoint as it involved a moral code. If the universe itself had a mind there would be no good and evil, it would only be action and reaction.

I had thought about that on many occasions, and tried to mimic that attitude, but ultimately, love and hate for something, even if it wasn't part of the immediate thought, drove me to do everything in life.

I'd taken many lives away, lives that forced pain and suffering upon the weak, yet I had never given a life back to the universe. Linda… If we were to have a child I would have the opportunity to begin replacing what I had removed… one bad for one good, one child at a time; that would be a thing of beauty, a thing to be proud of.

The more I considered it the more I realized I was merely justifying my actions from a very subjective standpoint. I was being absurd.

After a while the pot began to wear off and I considered taking another hit from the joint I'd rolled. However, I had also read about eating marijuana and was eager to try it. Many claimed that it was a different kind of high, that it would take you on an entirely different journey.

I went upstairs and got a large glass of water and brought it back down into the basement. The bud I had broken up was sitting on the workbench in front of me. I wasn't sure how much I should swallow, especially for my first time, so I took about a tablespoon and put it into my mouth. The taste was very unique, nothing like I had tasted before. I raised the glass and drank all of the water, pushing the marijuana down my throat.

I didn't feel anything for about an hour, and then very quickly it hit me like a hammer. I wasn't hallucinating in the sense that I was seeing things, but I was seeing things differently. The weight bench across the room from me no longer made sense. It wasn't truly a solid structure; it was simply atoms trapped in a location until the inevitable corrosion process slowly freed them over time.

I walked over to the weight bench, running my hand across the cool, smooth metal. As I studied it an impulse came over me to get underneath the loaded bar supported by the bench. I pushed and the weight left the structure. I could feel my shoulders, triceps, and chest tighten. My mind was in control of everything, every move. I could either hold it up, or lower it down, anything I wanted. I commanded my body to lower it to my chest, and it responded instantly.

The weights clanked loudly and sounded alive as I raised the bar. I was their father, and the weights were my children, laughing and cheering, playfully demanding to be thrown into the air over and over. I pushed the bar up, and then lowered it down many times, and as I did the lactic acid began to burn my muscle tissue and a bead of sweat trickled down the side of my forehead. It was fantastic. The stimulation was like nothing I had ever felt before. It was more intense, and more personal. I understood how my organism worked.

When I finished with the weights I sat up and stared at the floor. As I studied the concrete beneath me my skin began to rapidly secrete sweat. Soon my clothing was soaked. I stripped down naked, wringed out the wet shirt, and tied it around my head to keep the salty water out of my eyes.

The basement felt alive. Everything had a vibration to it and I wanted to explore the possibilities further. I walked over to the workbench and looked over the many tools I had collected over the years. Various hammers, knives, pliers, clamps, speculums... there was so much to choose from.

The scalpel sliced effortlessly across my chest. It was a bizarre sensation. I had been expecting my mind to register the cut as severe pain, but I felt very little. As the skin opened up I could see a thin layer of fatty tissue and then the muscle. Though I wanted to explore further I stopped. I did not want to have to go to the doctor to have it stitched up. A small wound I could take care of, but anything much larger would require a professional.

I took the small sewing kit from underneath my workbench and sat on the floor with it. After wiping the flesh and the needle down with alcohol I began stitching the wound shut. The piercing of the needle was painful but the idea of fixing myself was incredible and drowned out the sting. Blood slowly crept down my chest, then my fingertips, eventually finding its way to my wrist. The sight was something special. I could damage or repair my structure at any time. I was in control.

After closing the wound and wiping myself off I laid on my back. The concrete was cold against my naked flesh, yet refreshing. I knew that I would not be fully sober until the morning and that I could not forget about delivering food to Linda.

As I thought about what food I would pick out for her my genitals began to tingle. With the assistance of the marijuana it was not difficult to imagine Linda's mouth sucking and pulling at me. I became aroused and started to fondle myself. I could feel Linda's hair brushing against my thighs as her head moved up and down, her mouth fully engulfing me.

My heart rate picked up and my chest pounded as she went faster and faster. My lungs pulled and pushed air at a rapid pace and just as I was on the verge of losing consciousness, or so it felt like, a very intense and prolonged orgasm began to develop. It started deep within my stomach and washed across my body in every direction. I convulsed as it reached the tip of my cock and shuttered violently as I released. I had to pull my hand away. The pleasure was too intense and nearly made me black out.

I laid on the floor for long moments recovering from the intensity of the orgasm. The physical and emotional connection I had experienced was far beyond anything I had previously known. My toes and face still tingled and my genitals felt like they were being massaged with warm feathers.

Though I wanted to explore further I needed to clean myself up and set the alarm clock. I would have many more opportunities to experiment with marijuana.

After turning the shower on to let it warm up I walked over to the mirror. The stiches on my chest were seeping blood and trails that resembled streaks of lightning ran down my stomach and came to a halt at my pubic line. The heart pounding sexual episode hadn't let the wound close properly, yet somehow it added to the experience of it all.

I stayed in the shower for half an hour. The water crashed against my flesh and I turned the handle with the big H on it down almost all the way. The cold streams tightened my skin as they cleansed. I had never felt so crisp.

The process of drying off no longer annoyed me. The soft fabric absorbed the water with ease. Once I was completely dry the heated breeze coming from the air conditioning vent brushed my body hair and sent chills running all over.

It was only one a.m. so I set the alarm clock for ten. That would give me enough time to wake up and find a suitable meal for Linda. I pulled the sheets up to my neck and before long I was lost in a deep sleep.

Chapter 17: Exorcism

I had spent the previous six weeks reading about and experimenting with marijuana. I smoked it or ate it almost every day. I had finally started letting Linda stay the night at my house. I would make sure to ingest a small bud before she came over. It brought the relationship to a new level. My intense orgasms drove Linda mad with lust. She would send text messages to my cell-phone while I was at work, telling me about all of the naughty things she was going to do to me. It was perfect.

I wanted her to try out the marijuana as well but I didn't know how to bring it up. We had never discussed drugs and because she was such a kind spirited woman, she never spoke ill of those who used them, so I wasn't clear on her stance. However, something else had been on my mind as well; something that I could control.

I would lay awake in my bed, sometimes for hours, imagining what it would be like to dissect someone while using the plant. Three weeks after my first experience I began to plan out an abduction. I wanted to do an interview while both of us were under the influence and needed him to have multiple violent crimes on his record.

Thirty miles from my home stood the City of Camden. It was one of the worst cities in the country. Violence, murder, theft, rape, robbery, assault; the numbers per capita were staggering. It was in that city I would find my next project to work on. The area I would be searching in was notorious for being absent of police. They only came if they were called, and they were always late.

It took me days but I finally compiled a list of men who met the requirements I needed to justify my actions. They were all wanted for murder. Each victim had been innocent; a grocery store clerk, a baby sitter, and a grandfather who wouldn't give his car up. All three of the men had also been arrested for prostitution.

I had planned carefully. I called in sick on Wednesday and would not return until Friday.

Wednesday night approached and I told Linda I had a stomach flu and I was afraid she would catch it, so I wanted us to not have any physical contact until I felt better. She was upset but agreed that it would be better for her not to risk it. She was in her last semester of the nursing program and didn't want to take a chance of falling behind in her studies.

After putting the black bed cover on my truck I'd ordered through the dealership I grabbed a small bag of supplies and headed for the city. The streets were filthy and riddled with trash. Prostitutes stood on the corners and suspicious gang banger types walked about freely. I had to be careful as I was out of my element. I could easily be caught in a situation where I was outnumbered and outgunned. The only weapons I had available were chloroform and a wooden baton that I had modified so that it was disguised as a fancy umbrella handle.

I drove around for over an hour until I came across exactly what I was looking for. On one of the lonely corners stood a small group of transvestites smoking cigarettes and shivering in the cold. However, I had to be certain. I would never harm a woman; it had to be a man, and an evil one at that.

I pulled up slowly, keeping my foot away from the gas to keep the noise of my muffler down. One of the *girls*, a black man standing over six feet tall, approached my open window, smacking his gum and flicking his cigarette onto the sidewalk. He fit two of the descriptions of the men I was looking for. Their aliases were Sheana and La'trice.

"Hey sugar, you looking for something special?" His voice was high pitched and raspy.

"A friend of mine told me about a girl who works over here... said she has the nicest mouth this side of the city. Her names La'trice, have you seen her around?"

"You came to the right place baby. La'trice, right here, in the flesh." He said it with pride as he pointed to himself with both hands.

"Today's my lucky day; you're just as fine as he said you were. How much for a blowjob?"

"That's what I like, a white boy who is straight to it. It's fifty for the mouth, one-twenty-five for the ass, and everything else is up for negotiation."

"Sounds like a fair price, hop in."

He gave me directions that led us around the corner to an alley that he had obviously frequented. I pulled in slowly and then shut off the truck. La'trice fixed his wig and then looked over at me, his lipstick glistening on his yellow teeth.

"Go on sweetie, pull it out... don't be shy."

Everything was going exactly as I had planned. I opened my zipper and pulled my pants down to mid-thigh. As he leaned down over my lap, I stopped him.

"Do you mind if I drink this whisky while you suck my cock? It's kind of a fetish."

"Sure baby, you do your thing and I'll do mine, just don't spill it in my hair."

As his forearms rested on my thighs, his hands opening a condom wrapper, I opened the bottle of whisky which contained chloroform, and soaked the sponge I had up the sleeve of my jacket.

Just as he went to push my underwear aside I grabbed the back of his neck and shoved the sponge into his mouth and nose. He bucked wildly, ripping at my hands and kicking the passenger door. A few moments later he was out.

I pushed his body off of me in disgust and forced his head down between his knees. After spraying disinfectant all over my body and hands I left the alley slowly with no lights on and headed in the opposite direction I'd found him. Only four minutes away there was an old closed down restaurant I'd located on a realtors website. It had a small field behind it with a bunch of stripped vehicles and junk piled around. I pulled around back between two old trucks and got out.

La'trice weighed over two hundred pounds and was difficult to slide into the back of my truck. I stuck a racket ball in his mouth and hog tied him with tape. After securing his body tightly in place with cargo straps I put the bed cover down, locked it, and shut the tailgate. I had to hurry. It wouldn't be long before his friends were looking for him and I didn't exactly look like I was up to something legal.

The ride back was fairly uneventful. I could hear him trying to squirm around after about twenty minutes, but he had no chance of escape.

It was one a.m. when I got back to my house. I drove the truck around back and backed it up to the basement doors. After a quick glance around I opened them, and then the tailgate. The man looked terrified, his eyes pleading for me to let him free. I forced him to inhale more chloroform through his nose instead.

I unbuckled the cargo straps and dragged him down the basement stairs, securing the door behind me.

After putting on some southern rock I sat in a chair in front of the man while smoking a joint. A few minutes later he came to, his eyes were glassy and red. I spoke calmly and directly to him.

"If you promise not to start screaming, or spitting at me, I'll take the gag out of your mouth. Nod your head up and down for yes if you accept my terms."

He nodded up and down and as he did his wig began to slide off to the side. After putting on latex gloves I removed the tape and the racket ball from his mouth.

"I want you to answer some questions for me. If you cooperate I will release some of your bonds and allow you to sit up. I know you are in a lot of pain right now.

"OK... whatever you say, man." He said desperately,

"Is your legal name Noah Andrew Wallace?"

"Uh... yeah man, that's it..."

"Good. Noah, is it true that you killed a store clerk while committing a robbery? Do not lie or embellish the story. Tell me exactly what happened."

He began to sob and as the tears came out mascara ran down from his lashes.

"Please man, I didn't... Don't kill me man, just let me go... I swear to god I won't say shit, man!"

"Noah, I need you to stay calm. If you are straight with me I'll be straight with you."

He hesitated and then went on, telling the story through slobbery whimpers.

"Man, fuck... I just got out of jail for hookin... I didn't have no money, and my grand-mama said she didn't want no faggots livin in her house. I was desperate... I tried to borrow from friends but they were all broke too. After two nights out on the street I had only eaten one time... I had to do something..."

"Please, go on..."

"...I stole a kitchen knife from my grand-mama and walked around for hours... I finally worked up the nerve and went into the grocery store... It was early in the morning and wasn't nobody around. It was just the clerk by himself... I walked through the line and put some gum on the counter... He started ringing it up and I pulled the knife and told him to open the register. His hands started shakin and he started buggin out.... I walked around to the side of him and told him again to open the register... He froze up and started crying real loud like a baby.... I got scared, man... I didn't want nobody to hear so... I panicked, man... I grabbed his mouth and tried to hold it shut but he clamped down and bit my fingers..."

"And then... what happened, Noah? What did you do?"

"I stabbed him in the back... and he fell down... and he... he just fuckin died man..."

Noah cried loudly as he finished his story, mucus dripping from his painted lips as he did.

"Noah... Did you know that the person you killed was only seventeen years old?" He shook his head no, snot dripping from his nose as he did.

"It's true. His name was Amari Prasad. He was an honor student and had hopes of going to medical school... But that won't be possible now because you murdered him... and you didn't even get the money."

"I'm sorry! I didn't want to hurt nobody, I just needed to eat... I was homeless, man! Do you know what that's like?!"

"Calm down, Noah... Shh... I feel that you have been honest with me and I am going to reward you for it. Follow my instructions exactly and I won't hurt you. If you try to escape or attack me... I will kill you. Do you understand?"

Noah nodded and put his forehead on the floor as he sobbed.

"I'm going to cut the tape from your ankles first and place them in shackles. Next I'll free your hands. After your hands are free I want you to slowly place them behind your head and interlock your fingers. Do you have any questions?"

He shook his head no and kept his face on the floor.

After removing the tape I locked his feet together and then put handcuffs around his wrist. He didn't try to fight me, or even look at me. I had a hammer in one of my hands as a safeguard.

"Good, now roll over on your back and sit up. You can lean your back against the wall."

He did as I said and sat there, his cheeks swollen and blotchy.

"Yo man, what are you gonna do? …Please, let me go!"

"Noah, do what I tell you to do or you are not going to like it. Take this chain, and these two locks, and secure one end to the handcuffs, and the other to the shackles." I slid them across the floor and they stopped at his feet.

The chain reaching from his wrist to his ankles was only a foot long. It would allow him to have a conversation with me in comfortable fashion without putting me in danger.

"Do you smoke marijuana, Noah?"

"Uh… yeah, sometimes…"

"How about eating it?"

"…No …I never did that."

"I am going to slide this bud over to you. I want you to chew it and swallow it."

I sat in the chair staring at Noah as he ate the marijuana. He gagged when he tried to swallow it but eventually took it all down. After consuming the bud he looked up at me and screamed out.

"Alright man I fuckin ate it! Let me go! Please!"

I lifted the hammer and put a finger to my lips, hoping he would take the hint seriously. I didn't want to cause him any unnecessary harm. There was much to be discussed, and I needed him to be healthy and coherent for our conversation.

I was still high from the joint but decided to eat a small bud as well. Noah stared at me as I chewed it, looking both confused and terrified at the same time.

"Now we wait."

After an hour or so I started feeling the effects. I was more used to it and had experimented with several different dosages. I could better control how deep I wanted to go. Noah was also showing signs of intoxication. He would nod his head back and forth and then stop, blinking rapidly and rubbing his face with his hands. He was ready to be interviewed.

"Noah, tell me, what was the first crime you ever committed?"

He hesitated, drooling as he stared at me with a panicky demeanor. He then spoke slowly. His throat made a gargled sound as he did.

"Man, my heart is beating too fast… I can't feel my feet or my hands…. I'm freaking out… I feel sick man! What the fuck is this?!... Please… help me…"

"Answer the question. What was the first crime you ever committed? Go on, talking will slow your heart rate down. You'll feel better."

"OK…ok… I was sixteen… I think. At school, everyone had been calling me a faggot and all sorts of other names for a long time… After a while I just couldn't take that shit no more. We was in the locker room after p.e. and some Mexican kid came up and spit in my face… He said some shit like "I bet you wish that was cum, huh?" Everyone started laughing, and calling me a bitch-nigga, and a pussy… I started crying… and the more I cried the more they picked at me, slapping me in the back of the head and shit…

"I snapped... I took the pad lock off of my locker and put it between my fingers. The Mexican kid asked me what I thought I was gonna do... and I showed him... I hit him in the head with it over and over and he fell down... Blood started coming out but I didn't stop... I kept hitting him until his boys jumped on me and beat me unconscious..."

Noah put his head down as he finished, sucking mucus back into his nose and wiping his eyes. I was intrigued. Bullies did deserve to be punished and his actions were justified.

"What was your punishment for beating the boy who picked on you?"

"I was expelled from school... The kid I busted up had to have forty stiches put in his head and was in a coma for over a week... The police came and picked me up from the hospital. None of the other kids who saw it told the truth... they said I just attacked him. The cops didn't believe my story. I cried and begged and told them everything, and they didn't give a fuck... Anyway, I was never allowed back at that school, and I had to spend four months in a boy's home..."

"Noah, is the boys home where you first experimented with the same sex?"

He was not pleased with my question. He jolted, slamming his back against the wall and crying out. I stared at him, refusing to entertain his outburst with emotion or threat.

"Yeah man, is that what you want to hear? Yes, that was the first time I had sex with a man."

"Was it with one of the adults that worked at the facility?"

Noah nodded his head up and down.

"Were you forced?"

"...No... more like talked into it"

"You said the other children at school called you a faggot. By the sound of your story, I assume that you were always attracted to men?"

Noah began to laugh as he spoke.

"Yeah man… While otha niggas were talking about how fine the girls in TLC were, I was thinking about Denzel Washington… I knew early on that I didn't like girls. Their "area" was gross to me… I didn't want no part of it."

"Do you feel like your chosen path of sexuality… the hurt you experienced from others for being gay… did that have a part in you committing more violent crimes?'

"Yo man, I aint gay, I'm a transvestite. There is a difference."

I remained calm, not wanting to offend him further. I didn't want to come across as if I was attacking him for his choice. His preference was irrelevant; it was the reasoning that mattered.

"Can you tell me the difference?"

"Man… A gay dude dresses like a dude, and he is attracted to other dudes. I'm a transvestite. That means that I was born with the mind of a woman… I dress like a woman, talk like a woman, and I feel like one too. That is the difference."

"The pressure you received from those around you… the insults… do you feel that they made you more violent?"

"Man… I guess."

He sighed as he said it, knowing that it was in fact true.

"Why did you stab that woman in front of the liquor store last year?"

"Man… how do you know all this shit?"

"Please, answer the question."

"That bitch… She was supposed to be like a pimp or some shit, but she was weak. Her and her two brothers would sit in the car across the street from where we were hookin and watch us. They were going to protect us if any crazy shit went down, and flash their lights if they saw any cops or heard them on the scanner. We paid them for like three weeks. Anyway, that bitch came up asking for money and I didn't have any so she slapped me. I was high on crank and I lost control. I stabbed that bitch twice with a nail file before her brothers ran me off."

"The police were called but she refused to give up your name; did her brothers ever try to find you?"

"No. The two brothers got locked up for drugs or some shit and that bitch is afraid of me... Hey, listen man... Where are you going with all this shit, what the fuck is this?"

I hesitated, but was growing tired of his outburst. I had extracted enough information for the experiment.

"...Noah... do you feel like you deserve to live after committing murder?"

He panicked. I still had the hammer in my hand and his eyes were locked on it now. I could see that the marijuana he had eaten was in full effect. The talking had eased his symptoms as was expected but my question brought him back to reality. Without warning he jumped forward on his hands and feet and leaped at me, grabbing for the hammer as he landed. I stepped backwards, pulling the hammer from his reach and Noah fell on his face, sobbing like a child as he lay there.

I had discovered that eating marijuana had quite a different effect on me than smoking it did. I was better able to simulate sympathy and compassion. Though I could have listened to more of Noah's stories I knew that he would only be thinking about dying from that point forward. It would be difficult to get the full truth from him, as he would try to victimize himself in order to receive mercy. The first part of the experiment was over.

Noah rocked back onto his knees and pleaded with me. I considered not going through with the rest of the plan, but that would create the risk of being caught. I decided that it was time to initiate the first phase of dissection. I instructed him to turn around and sit back up against the wall. As he turned I smashed the right side of his jaw with the hammer, knocking him unconscious.

I placed Noah on the *operating table* and secured his arms, legs, and torso with leather straps, carefully removing the previous restraints as I did. I then removed his female clothing with a knife and threw them to the side. I decided to leave his makeup on and cleaned the rest of his body thoroughly with bleach before beginning the procedure…

For reasons still unknown to me I hesitated before making any cuts. That case was different than the others. Perhaps it was the marijuana… To put it simply, I had a sense that what I was doing may be wrong. However, that was not enough to stop me. His screams made my hands shake as I mutilated his body beyond recognition. It was unlike anything I had ever experienced. The smell of his insides, the texture of the organs, the simplicity and complexity of the body… It truly blew me away. The marijuana complimented the procedure and took everything to a new level. It was a sensation that, in time, I would enjoy again.

Chapter 18: Fortitude

It had been months since I started smoking marijuana and the day that I was hoping wouldn't happen finally came. I received a phone call from the dayshift supervisor, Bill.

"Hey, Sully, we got a call from the orderly room. They want you to come in at two p.m. on the dot. They didn't specify why. You will be paid your normal wage and allowed to leave early. Cool?"

In a groggy voice I replied "No problem, Bill. I'll be there on time."

I knew that meant one thing and one thing only, a urinalysis. It was nine a.m. which meant I had about four and a half hours to thaw out the urine, slowly heat it up, and poor it into the I.V. bag that would be my bladder for the first part of the afternoon.

I headed down to the kitchen and followed the instructions I had printed out to the last word. I had confidence that the procedure would go nice and easy. Many others on one of the marijuana message boards I frequented had had great success with it.

As the temperature of the pot increased the unmistakable stench of piss filled my entire home. I waited patiently for over an hour and constantly checked the temperature. Finally it hit around ninety-five degrees. I didn't want to increase the heat too rapidly for fear of disturbing the balance of the urine. It went smoother than I expected and I still had three hours to kill until I needed to shower and head into work. I dumped the piss down the drain thinking it would be better to do it right before I left so that the urine would be as fresh as possible.

I ran back upstairs and dug through my closet for the dildo I'd bought to match my flesh. After throwing some DVDs and clothes to the side I finally found it. There it was in all of its glory, a four inch, floppy life saver. I tore the package open and felt the material with my hand. It was unlike the other toys that I had bought for Linda. It felt real and responded well to the touch. Not too soft, yet not too rigid. From two to three feet there was no way anyone would be able to tell the difference.

After locating the still packaged I.V. bag with the still attached mocha colored penis, I laid it on the bed next to the correct color penis. It was something I should have done long before. I needed to swap the two of them out. I removed the I.V. bag from the packaging and examined the attachment. It was a simple design. The plastic tubing would carry the fluid out of the bottom of the bag and through the device. *Simple enough.* So I thought, until I tried to remove the mocha colored penis. It was securely attached to the tubing with some type of powerful adhesive. I had to go online and find out what the adhesive was and how to soften it. Luckily, I found an article that said placing the product in hot water for an hour should do the trick. I did as was instructed, patiently waiting. Finally an hour had passed. It resisted at first but finally started to give. After a few minutes I had it all the way off and the tube appeared to be undamaged.

Next I had to create a hole inside of the flesh covered dildo. It proved more challenging than I had anticipated. The material was soft, and trying to put an ice pick through it was not working well. I was running out of options and then it hit me. I would light up the end of a metal hangar and burn a hole straight down the center. After heating the hangar up with a lighter I tested it on the base. It ate right through the material leaving a neat hole, but cooled quickly. It took me about twenty minutes but I was able to finally burn a hole from the head, down the shaft, and into the scrotum. I slid the tubing through the hole with some of the anal lubricant that Linda and I had been using and then washed everything off. There were a few visible burn marks on the head but I carefully snipped them away. When I was done I stood back and looked at my fully functional device. Though it was ridiculous it was also an excellent idea. I knew it was going to work well.

I stopped drinking water around twelve p.m. so that I wouldn't actually have to piss once I arrived. At twelve-thirty I began heating up the new batch of urine and hopped in the shower.

The time was near. It was one-thirty and my urine was up to temp. I poured it into the I.V. bag, strapped it securely to my thigh and snuggly against the under part of my scrotum. Next I put on the jockstrap-like device that kept the penis in place and connected the tube running from it to the I.V. bag.

Knock Knock... The door behind me opened.

"Hey, John, it's Jim, the landlord."
God dammit...

He saw me through the kitchen window and let himself in. Though he had a key I had locks on the interior to keep him out. He had always called before. How was it possible that I forgot to lock the fucking door? I was getting sloppy. That would never happen again. I had no time to react.
"Ah cool, you got one of those piss things, saved my son's ass last..."
"Jim..."
"Its cool, man, I smoke too. I'm not gonna say nothing, buddy, don't worry about it. I just came by to ask why you hadn't paid the water bill. You having money problems?"

My landlord was a decent person but a bit intrusive. I trusted that he would keep his silence.

"Sorry about that, Jim, it must have slipped my mind. It only comes quarterly so on occasion I forget. I'll pay it tomorrow morning, you have my word."

He smirked at me.

"No big deal, its only two weeks overdue, they sent me a letter so I wanted to check up on it... Woah, what's with all the locks on the basement? Are you keeping hostages down there?"

He laughed obnoxiously and slapped me on the shoulder, my pants still down at my knees. The dildo jiggled from the force of his hand.

"Jim, I'm sorry, I have to head to work and use this thing, I need to leave now, I'll catch up with you later, and don't worry, I'll pay the bill."

"It's cool man, I'm not worried about... Oh yeah, I'm heading out of the country to Greece for a few weeks. If anything goes wrong just give my son a call. I'll seeya, buddy."

I waved to him as he left and shut the door behind him. I was glad he didn't ask any other questions about the basement. However, that was something I would need to address as soon as I got home. Though he wasn't nosey, it did look a little suspicious. I had told Linda that the basement was filled with building materials and that the landlord was finishing up some work down there. She never even brought it up, I just explained it to her the first time she came to the house. I would need to move the operation somewhere else and clean that place out. I had no more time to think about that, I had to get to work.

It was around one-forty-five as I rushed out the door. I cranked the heater all the way up in my truck and kept my legs together as tightly as I could without putting the I.V. bag at risk. I showed up at the orderly room at one-fifty-eight. I should have been fifteen minutes early but, fuck it, I had made it. The lady at the front desk greeted me, took my information, and then told me to report to the clinic on base. I hopped back in the truck and headed over as quickly as I could without getting pulled over.

After entering the clinic I walked carefully toward the waiting room I had visited a few times before. Upon entering, the distinct smell of disinfectant masking piss filled my nostrils. I signed in at the desk and waited for my turn. I saw two "cock watchers" as we called them alternating in and out of the bathroom. One was a twenty-something lieutenant who was clearly disgusted with his assignment and the other was an overweight staff sergeant, the kind of guy who couldn't wait to watch people piss to get out of work. I was hoping I would get the lieutenant so no questions would be asked, hell, he probably wouldn't even watch me. I wasn't so lucky.

"Mr. Sullivan, right this way, sir."

The fat Sergeant waved his hand as if he was a butler as I walked passed him into the restroom. I could tell he was the kind of asshole who would get a little too close and take his job too seriously; however, I had no real way to combat that.

"Mr. Sullivan my name is Sergeant Rains. I need you to stand facing me the entire time you are urinating so that I can confirm that there are no hidden devices in use and that you are not attempting to dilute the urine with any chemicals. Wash your hands, dry them completely, take this cup, open the lid, and make your best effort not to spill any. You may begin when you are ready."

I did as was instructed. After washing my hands and drying them I unzipped my pants, pulled out the head of the dildo, placed it on the edge of the cup, and hit the switch on the tube that was located just to the side of my testicles with my pinky. As I pissed Sergeant Rain's brow lifted and he began speaking.

"Wow, your urine is much clearer than most peoples. It seems like everyone who comes in here is hung over and their piss is a more yellowish-brown color. You look like you are in pretty good shape; do you hit the gym a lot? I haven't seen you at the base gym, I go there a lot. I can't do much but ride the stationary bike because of my back but, I try to stay in shape…"

I interrupted him.

"Sir, I would prefer if we didn't talk while my penis is out in the open. I don't mean to offend but… it isn't something that seems normal to me. Thank you."

The Sergeant peered at me and then slowly nodded his head up and down. He disgusted me. He was the typical lazy scum that wasted tax dollars… but, I supposed someone had to stare at cocks all day. Everyone had a purpose.

After finishing I closed the lid, placed it on the counter, washed my hands as I was instructed to do again by the Sergeant, and headed for the desk where I would turn it in. With a gloved hand, the woman behind the desk took it, put a paper tape seal over the top, initialed it, and sent it to the back room. With that, I was gone. I had successfully used the device.

I was supposed to report to my work center immediately after, but I had to run back to my house and drop off the device. In the process I spilled a few ounces of the urine on my pants. I didn't want to be gone too long so I absorbed it the best I could with a kitchen towel and headed back in.

The day started off normal; smashing away at metal with a hammer, shooting rivets in a repair, bending tubing, that is, until one of the new kids drilled a hole through his hand. He was standing at the work bench across from me fiddling with a training project. I hadn't been paying much attention to him until he started screaming for help. I was the only one around so I put down my equipment, took off my safety glasses and headed over to him.

His palm was ripped wide open, yet the drill bit was still somehow tangled in his flesh. His muscle and fat tissue was clearly visible. By the way his hand was contorted it was clear that he had severed at least one tendon. I knew that sight all too well. Soon after, the shift supervisor and the other desk jockeys ran over. One of them started getting sick to his stomach, another could hardly look at the gore, and the shift supervisor was stuttering and stumbling trying to figure out what to do. It was a situation that I had mentally prepared for on my many drives to work. I took command. I pointed at the shift supervisor and spoke clearly and decisively.

"Sergeant Moore, call an ambulance, now."

I then turned toward the other two and instructed them to go away if they could not remain calm. They both stepped back about fifteen feet and watched from a distance. The kid was in agony. Saliva dripped from his mouth as he screamed out in pain. I didn't think I would be able to bring him much comfort, but I would be able to help him.

"I need you to sit down on the ground and put your hands in your lap. I will take the drill from you and hold it in place. I am going to release the drill from the bit to take the weight off of the injury. Kid, look at me…"

He looked at me with terror in his eyes knowing that the weight of the drill was causing the most pain. We would be able to leave the bit inside of his hand without causing further damage. He nodded at me and closed his eyes. By then about fifteen people stood around us. No one interrupted me, everyone was just silent, some walking away, getting queasy from the strong iron smell the large pool of blood was producing. I could feel it soaking into the knees of my jeans.

"Ok, kid, be tough, this is only going to take a second."

Quickly and carefully I took the chuck key and rotated the lock until the drill released from the bit. At that moment a violent spurt of blood shot from his hand and splattered against my throat and face. With both hands I placed pressure around the wound and controlled the bleeding. He began to hyperventilate. He was hurt pretty bad. If I had to guess there was a good seven or eight ounces of blood already on the floor.

"You, bring the first aid kit and a paper bag out of the tool crib."

The guy I pointed at did as was instructed and came running back with the items.

"I'm going to hold this bag over your mouth, it will help you calm down. Trust me, I want to help you."

He didn't look at me he just nodded and began to breathe into the bag as I held it with one hand, the other keeping pressure on his wound. I then instructed the shift supervisor to hold the gauze from the first aid kit firmly in place on either side of the drill bit. I continued talking with Airmen Farley until the paramedics arrived and took over. After they secured a legitimate bandage around his hand they rolled him away in a wheelchair and off to the hospital.

Everyone just stood around murmuring about the large pool of blood on the floor and hoping the kid would be ok. One of the supervisors came over with the biohazard kit and sprayed disinfectant on the bodily fluid. He had a large wad of absorbent towels in hand; the heavy duty kind made for hydraulic fluid, but had to turn away. He told me he was lightheaded and handed me the towels. I grabbed a pair of latex gloves from the bio kit and sopped up the mess. Afterward I took the waste and placed it in a large trash bag and carried it out to the dumpster. On the way back in I stopped by the restroom and cleaned all of the blood from my face and hands. Luckily no one was in there, I didn't feel like explaining a thousand times what had happened, I just wanted to get changed and get back to work.

When I came back to the shop I was asked to fill out an accident report. I gave every detail that I saw, signed it, and went back to my bench to finish the repair I had been working on.

An hour later I had mostly forgotten about the incident and was thinking of Linda. As I grinded away at the metal I was becoming lost in the sparks while imagining her soft hands caressing me. My fantasy was interrupted by a man calling my name. I put down the tool and took off my safety glasses. There was a Colonel in his dress blues standing behind me. A very tall, and too clean for real life, Arab looking man in his mid-fifties.

"Mr. Sullivan..."

He extended his hand to introduce himself. His voice was unusually deep; it didn't really match his overall persona.

"My name is Colonel Rogers. I was briefed by your Flight Chief about the accident that took place today. We are all very impressed with you. You took control of the situation. Airmen Farley was in good hands. We've been in contact with the hospital and they confirmed that one of his tendons was torn in half but, they may have a chance at saving it, he'll just be out for a while.

"I'm glad the kid is going to be alright... I appreciate you coming by. I'm still a little in shock over the whole thing...

I was lying, I had seen much, much worse. I wanted to get back to thinking about Linda.

"As we all would be... There is a commander's call tomorrow at three p.m. at the base theater. I know it isn't typical for civilian employees to attend, however I would like to publicly thank you and give you an award. Will you be able to make it?"

Fuck... The last thing I wanted to deal with was an award ceremony; a thousand dead eyes staring at me as some campy pre-planned speech was delivered. However, if I declined it wouldn't look good. Getting awards also led to promotions and many times networking opportunities would take place after the ceremonies. Though I was relatively content with my financial situation I wanted more for Linda. She came first. I would show up, play the game, and look for opportunities.

"I'll be there, sir."

He shook my hand again and walked away with the Chief that had been standing behind him. The rest of the evening went by smoothly. I got off work around ten p.m. and headed straight to the house. The security of the basement had been in the back of my mind all day and I needed to take care of that problem soon. Linda had been coming to the house, and with my landlord coming in and making a joke about it, it just felt too risky. I would need to get rid of the sulfuric acid, janitorial bin, sound absorbent liner, medical tools, and a few other things. Everything else could be passed off as hardware or home cleaning supplies. I would set up second-hand furniture in front of the wood burning stove to make it appear as if it was a winter time relaxation spot.

I woke up early to handle the basement problem. It took me hours to remove the sound absorbent liner, remove the steel plate from the basement door, and dispose of the sulfuric acid. I was fortunate that behind my house were dense woods as far as the eye could see. I walked out about a hundred feet with a shovel in hand and started digging. At first the top soil and roots presented a problem, but once I got through that it was smooth sailing. In less than an hour I had dug what looked like a shallow grave. The barrels of sulfuric acid would fit right in, I'd cover them up, and that would be the end of it.

I took a long shower after the basement project had been completed. I had to focus on the ceremony. It was possible that I would be put in a situation where I needed to speak in front of the crowd. I would be vague, respectful, and humble. If I declined to comment it would come across as weak, as if I wasn't actually able to handle the situation. After getting dressed I headed to the ceremony and rehearsed a few lines that would likely be applicable to whatever the commander had to say.

It was two-fifty p.m. and the parking lot was packed. After finally getting a spot I hurried into the building. I was met at the entrance by my Flight Chief.

"Hey, Sully. Let's head on down to the front, I have a seat for you. The commander wants to address you first."

I nodded and followed him down to the front row. He fidgeted about and looked nervous for some reason. Perhaps he was afraid I would not be able to respond appropriately in front of the crowd. Though my personality had noticeably changed for the better over the last few months, I was still treated by most as a bit of an outcast.

The room fell silent. The Colonel's footsteps could be heard walking across the wooden stage just behind the curtain. His First Sergeant snapped to attention and belted out "Aten-hut!" and the entire room, including me stood up in unison waiting for the Colonel to put us at ease.

"Thank you all for coming out today... Please be seated... Before we begin I would like to recognize one of our civilian employees... As most of you are aware of by now, we had an incident here on the base yesterday evening. A young man, one of our Airmen, Airmen Farley from the Aircraft Structural Maintenance shop was involved in a severe accident, one that ended up costing him the use of one of his fingers. The doctors tried to salvage what they could, but the damage was too severe...

"When the incident took place, Mr. Sullivan, a fellow maintainer of ours was nearby. He heard the cries of pain and immediately went into action. Without hesitation he directed others on what to do in textbook fashion. I know it was difficult to see such a severe injury so unexpectedly, yet he was able to stay composed, remove the drill from the drill bit that was lodged in Airman Farley's hand, control the bleeding, and keep him calm and coherent until the ambulance arrived. It takes a lot of fortitude and courage to act as Mr. Sullivan did. Had he not been there in that moment the situation could have been much worse... Mr. Sullivan, would you please join me on the stage."

The crowd clapped loudly as I walked up the steps and over next to the Commander. I could see hundreds of eyeballs staring at me. It wasn't like I had expected. Many looked to be genuinely interested in the whole thing. I stood quietly with my hands behind my back and waited for my award.

"Mr. Sullivan I would like to present you with a coin. I've had this coin for over twenty years. It was given to me by my Commander after I had successfully performed CPR on an Airmen who had gone into cardiac arrest... He told me it was a hero's coin, that it was one of a kind, and that only a hero deserved to hold onto it. I will be retiring soon... Though I am saddened that one of our own was injured so severely, I stand proudly now as I pass it on to you…"

I took the coin with my left and shook his hand with my right. He had sincerity in his voice. An unusual sense of pride came over me as our hands met.

"Mr. Sullivan, do you have any words for our fellow Airmen and civilians in attendance today?"

He wasn't actually asking me, it was a polite way of giving me the floor. I turned, faced the crowd, and began speaking.

"It is rare in life that we get to help someone who is truly in need without having to seek them out. By chance, Airmen Farley and I were at the same place at the same time. I know that any person here would have done the same thing that I did, which was simply doing the best I could to help someone in need… I do not feel worthy of the coin I've been given, but I am honored to hold onto it. Colonel Rogers, thank you, sir, for the kind words."

I shook the Colonels hand and nodded my head towards the crowd as an eruption of near defining applause filled the room. The sensation was incredible. It was new and unique. It felt sincere. After the Commander had finished his thirty minute talk on safety, finances, and the current state of the war on terrorism we were all dismissed. I was met with handshakes and pats on the shoulder every few feet until I finally made it out to my truck. As I turned on the ignition my Flight Chief approached the driver's side window.

"Hey, Sully, why don't you go ahead and take the day off, it's a paid holiday for you… we'll take care of the paperwork... We're all real proud of you, man."

He didn't even give me time to decline; he just nodded and walked away. It all seemed like a bit much. The kid wouldn't have died, he just got hurt real bad, but that was the military way. There was no harm it I supposed.

Chapter 19: Variance

It was late February and cold as hell outside. Linda and I laid together on the large micro-fiber couch I'd brought down into the basement and placed in front of the wood burning stove. We had just finished making love and I was feeling very relaxed. However, Linda felt distant... something that had never happened before. She faced the other direction and stared into the flames of the open stove doors, silent and still. I didn't want to bait her by asking her what was wrong. If she had something to say I knew she would find the courage. She was likely putting it together in her head. Behind her, I waited patiently. A long time passed before she finally spoke, and I was glad she did. My curiosity was beginning to peak.

"John... I want to ask you something... You don't have to answer if you don't want to..."

"You can ask me anything, you know that." I caressed her hair and kissed her on the cheek as she spoke.

"What would you think about..."She began to cry, cutting her words short.

"Linda, what is it?" I expressed concern but wasn't too pushy in tone.

"Dammit! I'll just say it... Will you... Marry me?"

I was not expecting that question. I had often dreamed of marrying her, and even considered asking her on multiple occasions; however it seemed more logical to wait until we had been together longer and she had completed her schooling. I also did not want to rush into it and scare her off. Her asking me relieved all of that pressure. Of course I wanted to marry her. She had given me a reason to care about something other than myself and my own selfish urges. I was alive with her in my life. I mattered. I answered with a hint of playfulness to cheer her up and reduce her anxiety.

"You know, I was just about to ask you the same thing... I'd love to."

She burst into tears as she turned to face me. She kissed me so intensely I could hardly breathe. I didn't mind being suffocated under those circumstances. She was the most beautiful woman I had ever known. We laid there holding each other in comfortable silence until we drifted away.

Without a place to continue my other line of work since the basement was no longer a possibility, my marijuana smoking and ingestion had increased a great deal. My urges felt uncontrollable at times, but as long as I had Linda and my medicine I would be able to contain myself until I could figure something out. Or so I thought.

A new situation... a problem had presented itself that I didn't see coming. Linda's ex-boyfriend, a man she had never spoken about, was trying to make his way into her life again. They were engaged a few years back until he was arrested for beating her. She told me it was one of those "young and dumb" things.

When the police had arrested him they found a significant amount of meth in his house, giving him a sentence of four years. Somehow he had found a way to manipulate the system and was out early on parole.

Though he had a no-contact order he was sending her letters. There was no signature to identify him, and no fingerprints or DNA. The letters were vague, jumbled, and written to resemble poems. She was certain that it was him. The police could find no evidence that would directly link him to the letters. They believed that the stalker had no connection with him. They tried to comfort her by saying that many times the letters were meaningless and that people who had experienced similar situations had never been physically approached, that eventually the problem would disappear. I trusted Linda's instincts over the opinion of the police. They had done their best to end the problem, but months went by and there was no trace, no evidence, nothing.

I couldn't be with Linda every second of every day, even after she had moved into my house. She was still finishing up her nursing program and I had to work. I talked her into quitting her job and took over her bills.

I bought us handguns, a 380 for her and a 45 for me. I also made her carry around a panic button with a built in GPS. She was not to leave the house without either on her person. The local police were also aware of the issue and made sure to drive by the house often. They would also sit in the driveway to catch speeders. I didn't mind at all.

As time went on more and more letters came. We were supposed to give them to the police, but Linda would throw them in the trash, and I would collect them after she left for school. I wanted to know what kind of psychology I was up against. Was he just an addict living in the past? He had beaten her so I couldn't be certain what he would be willing to do. What if it wasn't him? Surely he would have slipped by then, he wasn't exactly a genius from what I was told. No, Linda knew it was. She had no doubt.

I was at my boiling point. Linda walked around in fear at all times; she wasn't able to sleep peacefully as she once did. It was heavily affecting our relationship. It ate at my soul. I wanted to destroy, to rip apart…

I still recall the last letter. I pulled it from the trash and studied it for long moments. It wasn't like the others. The previous letters did not indicate that the writer would be trying to physically contact Linda. They were jumbled, poorly worded nonsense. The last one was different. I remember it word for word…

Linda my sweet   Linda my love
Love! Pain! Sacrifice! Loyalty! Patience!
I have smelt it, tasted it, felt it. It is my dream.
I've thought of it on so, so many frightful nights.
Two hearts once connected… They will love again.
Your love is lost, so, so very lost. It yearns for me.
We will be together again and again, my love.
Do not run from me, do not hide, my love.
We are forever. You are mine, forever.
I will have you. I must have you.
The time is near. Be patient.
Love does not know time.
Love only knows us.
Wait for me.
Linda

I wanted to handle the problem immediately, but I was having difficulty finding the right circumstance. If I was not at work, and Linda wasn't at school, she was with me at all times. There was also the very high possibility that his disappearance would be connected to me. I had to be very careful. Doing a life sentence for murder would be worth it if it meant Linda would be safe. However, I knew the right opportunity would eventually present itself; I just had to be patient. I preferred to be by Linda's side than staring at her through prison glass.

Chapter 20: Hell

His name, Linda's ex, was Frank Gerald Scardino III. A construction worker and member of a biker gang called The Scorpions. After extensive research I found out that he had recently been released from the halfway house he'd been staying in and had moved in with his cousin, Carl "Carlito" Scardino, also a member of The Scorpions. I wasn't sure what information Frank had about me other than my address. I didn't know how far he would go or if he intended to harm either of us. It was a risk I would not take. I would handle the problem before it ended up on my doorstep.

Linda and her mother had flown out to California to lay her deceased aunt to rest. If I was going to fix the situation, that was my chance. I had been plotting for months and had a few ideas in mind. A month prior I'd drove past Carlito's house in the early morning hours. Quietly, I crept around the house and looked into the windows. In the living room is where I found them; Frank and Carlito, dead to the world. One was on the couch and the other on the floor. There were beer cans everywhere and some type of pipe on the table. It was probably for meth or crack; they were too rowdy to be potheads. That was the exact circumstance I would need.

It was Monday and Linda would not be back until the weekend. I paced around the house all day considering my options and planning my attack before heading into work. If there were going to be multiple people I couldn't make any mistakes. They were both large men, likely more than familiar with hand to hand combat, and certainly armed. If I lost the advantage at any point they would kill me, and Linda would suffer. That would not happen. It could not.

When I got off work I headed straight home and skipped the scheduled exercise session. I cleaned myself up and put on all black clothing. I sat patiently on the bed waiting for the clock to hit three a.m.

On the way to Carlito's house I went over the plan many times. No mistakes. No evidence. I would succeed. I had brought chloroform, a Zippo, and a large survival knife, the knife the Marine Corps used. I also had another bag full of disinfectant, rags, and a change of clothes. I would find them in a deep drunken sleep, enter the house, use the chloroform on both of them, kill them, set the house on fire, and that would be the end of it. If the circumstance looked any different, I would leave and come back another time.

It was four a.m. when I arrived. I parked my truck behind a dumpster down the street from Carlitos. After shutting off the engine I waited twenty minutes so that if by chance my truck had woken anyone they would have time to fall back asleep.

The small, tattered neighborhood was dead silent and the street lights no longer illuminated the area. Most of the houses showed classic signs of abandonment; boarded up windows, furniture in the yard, and cars on blocks. It was depressing. If anyone else did live there they were probably drug addict-squatters.

I put on latex gloves, pulled the ski mask over my head, grabbed the bag with the chloroform and Zippo inside, and carefully made my way through the darkness.

It was the same scene as the last time I'd stopped by. The house was quiet except for the cheap TV playing an infomercial. Carlito was passed out face-first on the floor and Frank was lying on the couch with a blanket over him and a bottle of liquor lying on his chest.

I went around to the side of the house where the kitchen was. I could still see them through the windows. I checked them all, looking for one to unlock. Not the first, not the second, but the third opened. I slid it upwards silently and climbed inside. My heart began to pound in my chest. I had not had to deal with two people before, at least not like that, but I had no choice. No one would harm Linda. I would do anything to make sure of that.

Slowly I crept over and stood behind the couch examining Frank. As I gently set the bag down and pulled out the chloroform something beneath his blanket moved. I froze, gripping the knife handle attached to my belt. A trashy looking woman with soars on her face emerged from beneath the covers. *Fuck.*

She sat up and yawned. After a brief pause she began looking around the room. I was hoping that she would fall back asleep and I would slip out the window. I was not so lucky.

Her gaze met my own as she looked into the mirror across from us that was on top of the fireplace. Her eyes widened and just as her mouth opened to scream I dropped the chloroform, shattering it on the tile below. I had no time to think. I grabbed her forehead and jammed the knife into her brain stem. She convulsed and shuttered. Frank and Carlito both sat up in a drunken haze. There was no turning back. The situation was sloppy and I had to deal with it.

As I pulled the knife from her neck Frank's head spun around. He jumped from the couch and stumbled over Carlito before crashing into the wall. Quickly I moved in his direction but was stopped short. Carlito grabbed my legs and pulled me to the ground. He began screaming.

"Who the fuck are you?! Kill this mother fucker! Kill him!"

Frank ran to the kitchen while Carlito and I struggled for control of the blade. He was a powerful man but I was able to put my knee on his neck and get the advantage. He pulled a knife from his boot and jammed it into the side of my thigh. It was deep. The sharp pain caused me to lose my holding.

We both scrambled to our feet. Carlito lunged at me, growling through clinched teeth. He pushed me back onto the couch and began smashing his fist into the side of my skull. I wouldn't be able to take much more. I was able to free my wrist of his other hand for a split second. I drove the knife into his rib cage and twisted it. He backed away and fell to the floor, grasping at the hilt with his hands as he groaned.

I stood up and went after Carlito to finish the job. Before I could do anything Frank came running at me with a butcher knife. I evaded the first swipe, the second slicing my forearm open. He charged at me over and over, swinging wildly; spit flying from his mouth as he attacked. I searched frantically for a weapon as I backed away. Carlitos knife was still in my leg, but if I pulled it out, and it had damaged an artery, I'd bleed out quick. I circled around the room evading Frank's assault. The situation was starting to look grim. And then, I saw it, my saving grace; a rusted machete lying on the tile next to the shitty TV.

After dodging another wild swing I jumped over Carlito and grabbed the machete. Frank and I stood there for long moments, neither of us making a move, both of us breathing heavily.

"What the fuck is this, man?! Who sent you!? Who fucking sent you?!"

I saved my breath and lunged at him. Frank backed up toward the wall, tripping over a table and falling down onto his back. I raised the machete and slashed it down toward his skull with great force. He raised his arm to deflect it causing the metal to disappear into his flesh. He whaled in agony as I chopped at him over and over.

His arm was all but severed and was no longer in the way. He pleaded with me to stop. It was hopeless for him. I continued slamming the machete into his body. The thought of him hurting my sweet Linda brought my wind back. I cut him from every direction, removing his left ear, nose, and a large portion of his scalp in the process. Blood splattered on the ceiling with each swing.

He no longer moved, only the faintest whimper could be heard. To my left Carlito laid on his back, his chest hardly rising with each desperate breath. It was time to finish it. I turned back to Frank.

"Frank... Frank, look at me!"

He lifted his head slowly. His eyes were coated in blood. He managed to whisper words through the gore filling his mouth.

"Who... arrre you?"

I removed the ski mask and kneeled down in front of him.

"My name is John Sullivan... I am here to kill you.

"...Who... wh-why?"

"You know who I am you fucking scum!"

"I d-don't... I swear..."

I should have just killed him, but it was personal. He had to understand why I was there. Maybe the drugs and booze were causing confusion.

"I am here on account of Linda. You have been sending her letters."

"Linda? I h-haven't... I don't know... Linda?"

I was overwhelmed with rage as my loves name passed his lips. I grabbed what was left of his hair and slammed his head into the tile floor over and over.

"Don't say her name! Don't you fucking say her name!"

Carlito's head rose from the shouting and looked in our direction. Hardly able to speak he pleaded with me.

"Ple...Please, don't fucking do this, man!"

I walked over to Carlito and stomped on his face until he stopped breathing. He wouldn't interrupt my moment again. I then removed the knife from his ribs and went back to Frank.

"Turn over you fucking piece of shit. Turn over!"

I grabbed what was left of his arm and forced him to his back. I placed a knee on his sternum, grabbed his hair with my left hand, and put the knife to his throat with the other. Blood bubbles and mucus popped in his airway as I stared at him.

"You know who I am; you know why I'm here!"

"I da-don't... I don't... Linda, I haven't..."

Fuck. Had Linda been wrong? I sat for long moments breathing heavily, trying to understand what was happening. Had I killed that woman for no reason? Frank deserved his punishment for beating Linda... But, if he hadn't written the letters, who was it? I felt sick, desperate, confused...

"Frank... I know you sent those fucking letters! Don't you fucking lie to me! Don't' you fucking lie!"

"What... l-letters?"

"The fucking letters! The letters you sent to my house! The fucking letters!"

"I... I don't... I didn't s-s-send any letters to anyone..."

I had no words. I looked at the dead girl next to me. She was probably harmless, just a victim of sexual abuse and drugs. I murdered her... My throat started locking up. A bizarre sensation came over me, one that had not occurred in my previous ventures. I was losing control of the situation, of my emotions. The heat from the tears rolling down my cheeks was sobering. My chin began to quiver as my hands shook. I was a murderer. I was the wolf.

I looked back to Frank. He didn't have much time left.

"It wasn't supposed to be this way, Frank."

As the pitiful whisper left my lips I picked up the butcher knife. Frank stared at me, his eyes barley open and his gargled breaths hardly audible. I pushed his forehead back and cut his throat from ear to ear in one motion. It was done.

I sat there for long moments looking at the three bodies lying around me. The room was coated in blood and stunk of iron and raw meat. I had to get out of there. I would have to deal with the emotions at another time.

I tore off my shirt and headed for the kitchen. I washed myself as quickly as possible at the sink, removing all traces of blood that I could see. After drying off with the dirty towel that was lying on the counter I used it to wipe down my pants and boots.

I had problems. My DNA was all over the place and I still had Carlito's fucking knife sticking out of my leg. I went back into the living room and removed the zippo from the bag I'd brought with me.

Quickly I moved around the house and lit all of the curtains on fire. I stood there for a moment as the ceiling filled with smoke, looking one last time at the mess I had created. The situation was much different than the others. I should have brought a gun, what the fuck was I thinking? Why did I cry? Was it the woman I killed? I didn't have time to think about it, I had to get the hell out of there.

I turned on the gas from the stove before bolting out of the house. The neighborhood was still quiet, but I could hear the faint rumble and cracking of fire behind me. It wouldn't be long until the house was engulfed.

I jumped into the truck cab and shut the door, desperately looking through my bag for the disinfectant. I poured it on my wounds and wrapped the rags over them as tightly as I could. I had no time to get dressed with the extra clothing. I started up the truck and headed back toward my house. I could hear the explosion behind me from two miles away.

On the ride home my adrenaline died down and the pulsating pain from my wounds began to set in. I had been stabbed, cut, and beaten. I had to get home and close the wounds. Nausea turned my stomach and I began rapidly blinking my eyes to stay conscious. I stepped on the gas, going faster as my condition worsened. I only had ten miles to go, just a few more minutes.

The unmistakable flash of police lights swirled in my rearview mirror. I was fading fast. The road ahead became a blur, and then blackness.

The last thing I remember was lying in the grass with a police officer kneeling beside me.

"Hey, stay with me man! Stay with me, the ambulance is on the way… You're hurt real bad, don't move, I'm here man, you're gonna be alright, just stay still… What's your name, sir?"

His words didn't make much sense to me. The only thing I could mutter was *Linda*.